Λ

DAN FANTE was born and raised in Los Angeles and is the son of novelist John Fante. At twenty, he quit school and hit the road, eventually ending up as a New York City resident for 12 years. Fante has worked at dozens of crummy jobs – door to door salesman, taxi driver, window washer, telemarketer, private investigator, night hotel manager, chauffeur, mail-room clerk, deck hand, dishwasher, carnival barker, envelope stuffer, dating service counselor, furniture salesman, and parking attendant.

Mooch is the second book in his Bruno Dante trilogy, picking up where *Chump Change* left off.

Praise for *Chump Change*

'a dirty, squalid and brutally compelling little tale ... his style is raw, insightful and deftly realised' *Time Out*

'Don't miss *Chump Change*. It is passionate, obscene and quite wonderful.' *Los Angeles Times*

'It gives an honest misfit's view of America far too few know.' *John Fowles*

'On one level, with the air and vapours of Fitzgerald on every page, this book might appear to be merely another account of America Hits the Bottle. But *Chump Change* is better than that, and its nihilistic undertones are offset by a genuine filial affection at its heart, and a wit which does not disguise the deathly kismet that is the boozer's lot.' *Literary Review*

'With the eye of Chandler, the verve of Bukowski and the possible veracity of Exley, this is cult American writing at its best. A brilliant, ferocious book.' *Caledonia*

'There is a desperate underlying humanity to this book ... impossible to put down' *Buzz*

'a brutal and stinking ride to the heart of the city of the dead ... a book that is almost perfect.' *The Crack*

Also by Dan Fante

Chump Change

Mooch

Dan Fante

First published in Great Britain in 2000 by
Rebel Inc, an imprint of
Canongate Books Ltd, 14 High Street,
Edinburgh EH1 1TE

10 9 8 7 6 5 4 3 2 1

Rebel Inc series editor: Kevin Williamson
www.rebelinc.net

British Library Cataloguing-in-Publication Data
A catalogue record for this book is available on
request from the British Library

ISBN 1 84195 069 6

Typeset by Palimpsest Book Production Limited,
Polmont, Stirlingshire
Printed and bound by CPD, Ebbw Vale, Wales

... he hath sent me to bind up the broken-hearted, to proclaim liberty to the captives, and the opening of the prison to them that are bound.

(Isaiah 61.1)

Chapter One

I HADN'T WRITTEN a word or a story or anything in months. And I hated my job. But that didn't matter now. Nothing mattered because of the heat. It took an hour for me to finally make myself get up, put on a shirt, and get ready for work. I'd been avoiding it since Thursday.

Outside on the burning, suffocating street, I yanked a new parking ticket out from under the windshield wiper of my 11-year-old Chrysler, then tore it into as many small pieces as possible, flinging it at the sky. I hated being back in L.A. I hated that I hadn't had a drink in months. I hated that I was losing my hair. I hated my job. I hated filtered cigarettes and rap music and Tom Cruise's big, stupid white teeth. And I hated the fucking Parking Violations Bureau.

Opening the car door to my Chrysler was a mistake. The contained force of what had built up in an automobile after several days in the sun in a heat wave with the windows up, hit me. Exploding stagnation, decaying vinyl, strangled dust. A clear warning to go back to my room.

I was running late, so I threw my canvassing book and my coupon demo packets across to the passenger side of the car, sucked in a gulp of the rancid oxygen, then stuck the key in the ignition.

Nothing.

I repeated the procedure. Nothing.

I switched the ignition back all the way to the left to see if the electrical stuff, the gauges and flashers and the other shit, were working. Still nothing.

Sweat was beginning to collect on my forehead and beneath my shirt.

I tried the key again a new way: wiggled it, jiggled it sort-of, hoping that the motor might catch. It had worked before – another time on some other car before my life had turned on me. But not now. Again nothing.

A man walked by.

He appeared to be on his way to his own car. Dressed for the heat wave. Carrying a briefcase and wearing a pair of neatly-pressed tan slacks and a floral, green-mostly, silky, Hawaiian, sports shirt. L.A. casual. I recognized this person as a home owner from down my block, with the wife, the dog, the table saw in the garage. We had seen each other on the street a few times but had never spoken.

As he came closer, his eyes met mine for an instant, then darted away. I knew why. He recognized me. I was one of the come-and-go residents of the sober-living apartment house on the corner. A shitsucking loser. I would live to be six hundred million years old and still never earn the word 'hello' from this citizen prick or his fat-butted wife who spent her afternoons digging in the garden.

Passing my car's side window, he slowed down, bending at the waist to steal a glance inside. Maybe, I thought, maybe he's wondering why another adult, dressed for work in a sports jacket, slacks and tie, would be sitting behind the wheel of his car in the direct sunlight on the hottest day of the year with the windows up and his motor not running, sweating, suffocating, wiggling his ignition key back and forth like a brain-damaged retard fuck.

I looked at my watch. It was 10.15 a.m. I'd never make the sales meeting.

Unable to think of anything else to do, I lit a cigarette. It was the last cigarette in my pack of Lucky's. I took a hit and watched the inside of the Chrysler fill with drifting rivers of smoke. I hated everything. God. Everything.

'This is Albert Berlinski. How may I help you?'

'Mister Berlinski, it's Bruno Dante.'

'Dante! What's up? Where've you been? You missed both of the demos we had scheduled for you on Friday night!'

'I've had car problems with my Chrysler again, Mister Berlinski.'

'Myrna had to "no-show" those presentations – call your clients, re-schedule everything herself. You never phoned in.'

For the last few days I had been reading a David Martin novel and staying in the coolness of my room because of my revulsion for door to door canvassing in the miserable heat and smog of my Glendale sales territory. 'I was waiting for my mechanic to finish another car before he could start work on mine,' I said. 'An engine job.'

'This is Monday, Dante. You've had three days to fix your vehicle. What time will you be in?'

'The goddamn thing wouldn't start again this morning.'

'Sooo . . . now what?'

'I don't know. Personally, I'm at a loss. Nonplussed. Befuddled.'

'Of course this means you won't be attending the sales meeting again. I'll have to tell Mister Fong.'

'I promise you I'll get the car squared away and be in by this afternoon. You have my word.'

Berlinski paused – the death pause – I recognized it immediately. It comes just before the words that tell you you're bumped. 'You know Dante,' he said, 'we're prolonging the inevitable here. Bring in your units and I'll cut you a final check.'

'Mister Berlinski, I just said that I'd be there this afternoon!'

'We totaled out the sales numbers this morning. Last month you were number twelve. Down from number ten.'

'I can count, Berlinski. I'm aware of that.'

'In May you were also number ten. You've been number ten twice and number twelve once. You also no-showed at the Track Selling Seminar last Saturday. Mister Fong himself brought that up to me during our strategy review. Not being there was a mistake.'

'I know I missed the seminar. I felt like rat shit missing the seminar. That seminar course was a vital component in my growth as an ambitious sales professional. I had a sincere desire to be there, believe me. It's my goddamn car.'

'Fortunately for the company, as I just said, the issue is now resolved.'

'Mister Berlinski, never buy a Chrysler product. They're hog excrement. No wonder the Japs and other alien conglomerates are taking over America. My car is further evidence of the demise of the fucking U.S. economy and the American dream. May I please talk to Fong personally on this?'

'It's my decision, not *Mister* Fong's. You're terminated. As of today. Bring in your units and your demo kit and the coupon books. I'll have Myrna total up what we owe you.'

'I'm being kicked while I'm down. I fucking-goddamn strongly suggest that you reconsider your decision.'

'How many units do you have in your trunk?'

'I've got the two Kirbys, a Hoover upright and the five hand-held Dirt Devils that were distributed to my team after the show. Eight pieces all together. What about another shot here, Mister Berlinski?'

'Bring the units in. I'll voucher them myself.'

'That's it? I'm fired?'

No answer.

'Well . . . okay, Mister Berlinski. But before you hang up, I would like to share something with you. Can I do that? On a man-to-man level? May I be permitted thirty fucking seconds of your valuable, priceless, sales-executive time?'

'I'm busy, Dante. I'm in the middle of figuring the totals for all three teams. We'll talk when you get here.'

'You and I have spoken a lot on the phone, Mister Berlinski. Sometimes two or three times a day. Sometimes more if I got lost on my way to a demo and had to stop at a pay phone for directions. Okay? Correct or uncorrect?'

'Bring the units in, Dante. I'll make sure you get your check.'

'I just wanted to say, Mister Berlinski, that almost every time after we've talked, after I've hung up, I'd get back in my car and I'd feel like I just finished interacting with a sour-faced sub-human cocksucker with the same empathy and interpersonal dexterity as one of the assholes behind the glass at the DMV Information Window. I regard you as a complete putz, Berlinski. I always have.'

'No demo units, no check.'

I looked through my pockets. I had four dollars. Enough for a newspaper, a new pack of Lucky Strikes, and a container of coffee at the 7–11. I went back upstairs to my dorm room, took off my jacket and necktie and slacks, and threw them at the wall.

Yesterday's shirt and my unwashed jeans fit my body like old friends.

On the floor in my closet on top of my father's hand-me-down Smith-Corona portable typewriter I found my Yankees cap with the big 'NY' on the front. I slipped the hat on as protection against the heat. Jonathan Dante, my father, had been dead for eleven months. He died broke, broken hearted, collecting a stinking Writer's Guild Pension and seven hundred and sixty-two dollars a month in Social Security. A forgotten screenwriter. I had returned here to L.A. from New York City to watch him die, to inherit this typewriter. Three months ago, my cousin Willie checked out too. Booze and an overdose. Crazy, fat Willie. Thirty-five years old. Two Dante funerals in less than a year.

Next to the typewriter, on the floor in the typing-paper box, was the only thing I had written and not thrown out since returning to Los Angeles: a short story called 'Compatibility'. Twenty-five pages. I picked the story up and looked at the wrinkled title page, then back down at the typewriter's bared black keys. They stared up at me like the eyes of frightened boat people. Hurling the pages back into the darkness, I slammed the closet door.

On the street, on my way to the store, I had an insight, a flash that penetrated my understanding. My real difficulty – my problem – wasn't my depressions or my drinking or my job failures or even the unarticulated fear that I was a fucking insane whack. My problem was people. And they were located everywhere.

Chapter Two

IN ORDER TO live at the sober-living house where I lived, I had to not drink and attend three Alcoholics Anonymous meetings per week. At these meetings, I would hear reformed alkies stand up and blubber on about how great and miraculous their lives were without booze and drugs. How wonderful their new job was and what gifts from God and all manner of preposterous, come-to-Jesus bullshit. How they were now able to form lasting relationships or patch up the old ones with their separated wives and girlfriends and how their children had stopped darting behind furniture and fleeing to their bedrooms when they saw them coming through the front door. Tra-la-la. Etcetera. So forth. Not my experience. I was not what AA's call a WINNER even though the WINNERS are supposed to be the people who haven't had a drink all day. I was not some transformed, anointed, cured gimp, tap dancing my way through life and thanking God and the Twelve Steps for keeping him sober and saving his ass. Recently, I'd heard Chickenbone, our moron, sober-living house manager, giving an AA peptalk to one of the miserable new guys who was two weeks off alcohol and rock cocaine. At the end of his lecture, he looked the kid in the face and said, 'You know boy, sometimes you're the windshield and sometimes you're the bug.' I hate hearing pig snot like that. AA is full of that shit. Philosophical one-liners that imply that life on life's terms has its ups and downs but will somehow all equal out in the end. Tell that shit to the guys collecting plastic bottles and soda cans pushing their shopping carts down Broadway in Santa Monica or the young kid I met at the Friday Night meeting who was out on bail after a his last 'slippy-poo'. He thumped his girlfriend in a blackout and is now about to be sentenced to five years because of the O.J. violence laws in California. Nice work God. Hail Mary, full of grace.

For me, going without booze for the last four months straight was the hardest thing I had ever done. I was sober and no better off than before.

My weekly rent for my dormitory room at the sober-living house was already three days late. I telephoned my AA sponsor, Liquor Store Dave, from the coin phone in the upper hallway. In AA a 'sponsor' is your support system, someone who has already worked the Twelve Steps and has been sober a while. Liquor Store Dave had dozens of recovering alkie friends. My hope was to catch a break and get a job recommendation.

After spilling my guts to Dave about getting bumped from Fong's Home Maintenance and letting him know about my rent situation, he made me endure a five-minutes sponsor lecture. In the end, he insisted that I be willing to surrender to his advice. 'You can't think your way into right acting, Bruno. You have to act your way into right thinking. Your Higher Power has to be your top priority. Recovery first, right?'

'Right Dave.'

I heard him leafing through his address book on the other end, looking for a number. Then he stopped. 'Didn't you once tell me that you were a writer too?'

'Probably.'

'I've got a friend who writes résumes. He has an office in Culver City. Used to be a serious drunk; a hot-shot genius like you.'

'I don't know anything about writing résumes, Dave.'

'What kind of stuff have you written? Bad checks? Ha ha.'

'Poetry – a short story now and then.'

'You the next Stephen King?'

'The last Bruno Dante.'

'Ever make any money writing, Bruno?'

'High two digits.'

'Ha ha.' Dave kept flipping through his address book. 'You used to do phone work, didn't you? Boiler rooms? Telemarketing?'

'In New York,' I said.

He stopped turning pages. 'Perfect. Okay, call this guy.'

I copied down the phone number of a friend of Dave's, Frankie Freebase. According to Dave, Frankie was a 'Winner'. He had over seven years of continuous sobriety and was now making good money at a phone sales gig. Then I was given more sponsor direction. Dave told me to write a letter to God asking for help in finding the right career.

What follows here is a copy of the letter I wrote after I got back to my room:

Dear God:
   Please help me to know what the fuck to do with my life and how to fix it.
   Sincerest personal regards,
   Bruno

When I was done, I folded the letter and stuck it in the fly leaf of the novel I had been reading, *Tap Tap* by David Martin.

After sitting quietly for a minute or two, a thought came to me. The AA Big Book on page eighty-seven calls this inspiration and spiritual guidance. The guidance I got was to go out to my Chrysler and try to start it again. I scooped up my car keys, went downstairs in the nostril-searing heat, and did what the guidance said.

Nothing.

No God. Not a fuck. Nothing.

Chapter Three

THE MINUTE HE came on the line and opened his mouth, I knew that Frankie Freebase was from New York City – the typical-type phone guy I had worked with a dozen times. Only more so, because he was an ex-drug dealer.

His questions came at me like Uzi machine-gun fire. When I said that I had six years of experience in phone sales, it didn't mean anything. But when I said my AA sponsor was Liquor Store Dave, it was as if I knew the secret handshake. I was in.

We talked more. Frankie talked. Non-stop. Twenty minutes worth of words, syllables, and paragraphs escaping his mouth like the Bosnia army fleeing nerve gas.

The company where he worked, Orbit Computer Products, was in the business of selling generic label computer printer ribbons and new and re-stuffed laser printer cartridges. They employed about seventy-five telemarketers. Frankie was one of the top salesmen. Orbit paid its people straight commission. No paid vacations. No 401-K's. The owner of the company was also a sober AA guy, Eddy Kammegian. Through Frankie Freebase, I got a job interview with Kammegian.

Leon, my room mate at the sober-living house, worked nights as a security guard. He came home, and I talked him into driving me to Olympic Boulevard in downtown L.A. to Fong's Home Maintenance. In Al Berlinski's office I turned in my coupon books, all the vacuums, and my demo kit. Berlinski inspected everything, counting each page of each coupon book to make sure I hadn't pilfered any of his precious fucking coupons. An hour later, I got my final check. One hundred and forty-three dollars.

Next morning at 5.30 a.m., as prearranged by Liquor Store Dave and Frankie Freebase, Frankie swung by my sober-living house to pick me up. I had slept for two hours. Standing on the front steps, I watched a new, racing-green Jaguar convertible pull to the curb. Frankie was slurping coffee from a Starbuck's 16-ounce traveling mug. Already wired.

I had my tie on, my sports jacket, and my only pair of good shoes. But I was a schlub compared to my ride. His tan double-breasted suit alone was easily worth a thousand dollars. And either his tie pin was fake glass or a four karat mug-me diamond.

It was still dark, and the streets were empty and wet with ocean mist as we zipped along on our way toward Santa Monica. Boiler rooms in L.A. get started early because of the 3-hour time difference for their East Coast customers. Frankie cranked up the sound level on a Zig Ziglar motivational CD. I had never heard Zig or anything else other than rap music played that loud before. A bank thermometer said it was already seventy degrees. In the distance, to the east, the sun was a wavy bubble just beginning to pulse up through the haze, peeking between the high rise office buildings in Century City. My mind, the firing squad, numb and dumb and tired, went into neutral for the rest of the ride.

Pulling into the company parking lot, Frankie tucked the ragtop Jag into his spot. My interview with Eddy Kammegian was set for six o'clock.

Orbit's offices were located in a deserted warehouse area

of Santa Monica near where the old Southern Pacific railroad used to dead-end. The company didn't look like much from the outside as we walked toward it across the gravel: a plain, older, freestanding, one-story concrete box. High up near the roof was a single row of opaque, wire-covered windows. The sharp incandescent lighting from inside was the only evidence of life.

We were stopped by a fancy security door that sported an elaborately-lettered gold sign. The sign read, 'Through This Portal Pass The World's Greatest Salespeople.'

To the right above the door frame was a blinking red alarm bulb. Frankie sliced a plastic card through a device and the light stopped blinking, changed to green, and the thick entry way clunked open.

Inside, everything was different.

Orbit was huge – dozens of partitioned-off desks and cubbyholes. The space itself was large enough to be an airport hangar.

Already I could hear the chatter of 'front' pitches and whoops of celebration from people closing sales. The room's intensity reminded me of the Stock Exchange in New York or Sunday afternoon at an Atlantic City casino.

Frankie pointed across the marketing area to an all-glass office overlooking the floor. 'Up those stairs, hotshot,' he barked. 'Remember, knock first. Kammegian don't like surprises.'

'Wish me luck?'

'Yeah, right . . .'

Eddy Kammegian's smile had as much sincerity as Bill Clinton's. Orbit's dress code was that all the males wore ties. The suits, like Eddy and Frankie Freebase, were the wheels, the bosses. The guys without jackets, the ones in plain white shirts with ties, were the regular grunts like me. Women at the company wore dresses or pants with blouses.

He was young to be as successful as Frankie said he was, middle thirties. Big too. Six-three or six-four, weighing at least two hundred and twenty-five pounds, with the look and moves of a nimble primate as he crossed the carpet to his desk. High forehead, hair cut short. Mark McGwire in a Georgio Armani pinstripe. Behind him on the wall were trophies and plaques and a lot of militaristic-looking shit and paraphernalia.

We sat down. His desk surface was the size of two mahogany coffins. The silence was so clumsy I had to talk. 'Shouldn't I be filling something out: an application?' I said.

The salesman's teeth were back. 'There's no paperwork to fill out, Mister Dante.'

'Oh, okay.'

More silence.

Now I smiled. 'So, how does your company hire people? Like this?' I asked.

'Just like this, Mister Dante. Exactly like this.'

'What about work history? References? A résumé?'

'My agenda in the interview phase is to create a relationship with each of our potential new Account Executives.'

'You interview everybody yourself?'

'Correct.'

I must have made a face. Kammegian noticed me doing it. 'That bothers you?' he asked.

'No. But most other companies this size have a department for hiring. Human Resources. Personnel.'

'Frankie tells me that you're new on the AA program. You moved here from New York?'

I nodded. 'Right. Correct. But I was born and raised in L.A.'

'And you have experience in telemarketing?'

'Yes I do. I have experience.'

'And you're "good" on the phone?'

'I'm okay.'

'Oh, just okay?'

'No, I'm good . . . I'm a winner.'

Kammegian's big body tilted back in his oxblood leather chair. 'Question, Bruno: What's your definition of "courage"?'

'"Courage", Eddy?'

'In telemarketing. In sales. Real balls.'

I noticed a gold or brass dish on my side of the desk. I took it for an ash tray. 'Okay to smoke?' I asked.

'Orbit is a tobacco-free environment.'

'Well – okay – I think courage in phone sales is being persistent, continuing to ask for the order – to keep closing until the mooch says yes. That takes guts.'

'I'd call that tenacity.'

'Whatever . . .'

'No, not *whatever*! Tenacity is an admirable quality, but it's not what I'm talking about. I'm referring here to genuine courage, Bruno.'

'It takes genuine courage to keep asking for the order, Eddy.'

'May I give you my definition?'

'Absolutely, Eddy.'

'The essence of true courage in any dynamic, proactive sales environment is a systematic sustained effort despite whatever obstacles one may encounter.'

'Right. Persistence.'

'Setting goals! Maintaining focus through the beginning days and months of massive rejection. Making call after call. Lashing oneself to the task of achievement, making the unshakable conscious decision to do and go through whatever is necessary to be a success. That's real courage. Front-line foxhole courage.'

'I hear what you're saying, Eddy.'

'No, Mister Dante, you don't. You're full of shit! You want a job with my company and I'm the boss so the astute thing to do is to agree with whatever I say. Sitting here now if I told you that my senior managers and I ritually put on flowing orange robes, shave our pubic hair, and drink chicken blood in the moonlight on Tuesday nights, you'd look across at me, smile, then nod your head approvingly.'

'I'm ready. When do I start?'

'Frankly Bruno, candidly, the person I see before me, across the desk, is a loser, a train-wreck. Your body language screams it. The smell of what you are is now stuck to the walls of my office like the odor of tenement piss.'

I was on my feet.

'Sit down, Dante. I'm not finished. You're sober how many days – thirty? Sixty?'

'What is this?'

'Sit down. Or leave. Take your choice.'

I stayed standing.

'In December, I'll be ten years off booze and drugs.'

'Con-grad-u-fuckin'-lations, Eddy.'

'You're here for a job, correct?'

'Yeah, but no one told me I'd have to suck your cock for it.'

'My top salesman earned two hundred-and-ninety-two thousand dollars last year. If that kind of income interests you, then sit down!'

I sat down.

'I ask the questions. You answer. Understood?'

I nodded 'yes' then changed my mind. 'So how about asking some of the ones that don't make the interviewee feel like a gulag inmate?'

The big man's smile was back. 'You should have seen your face just now,' he sneered. 'Your eyes had the expression of a stray dog loose on the freeway in rush hour traffic. Was that your success face?'

I got up. 'Know what Eddy – fuck this!'

Kammegian was up too, pointing. 'There's the door, bitch! Have a nice day.'

I wanted to move but couldn't. There was nowhere to go. I felt frozen. Instead, finally, I sat back down.

'Better,' he hissed. 'Now tell me how many phone sales jobs you've had in the past few years. What types of products have you sold?'

'What have I sold? . . . Everything. Why?'

'That's a non-answer.'

'Okay, name a boiler room hustle . . .'

'Let's narrow it down. What've you sold here in Los Angeles?'

'In L.A. I've sold vacuum cleaners door to door and a dating service. No phone stuff.'

'Why?'

I realized that I had nothing to lose. 'I was a flame-out at telemarketing,' I said. 'I wound up pounding vodka and snorting coke all day in the phone rooms where I worked.'

'How many telephone selling jobs have you had? Total?'

'I don't know. A lot.'

'My fuse is getting short, Mister Dante. How many?'

I ticked them off. 'Credit correction, guaranteed loans, hair restoration, rare coins, tools, office supplies, copier toner, oil and gas leases, knock-off feature videos, ad space, fund raising, porno, cable and wire, driveway cleaner, vitamins, internet website manuals, and discount long-distance. There's probably more. How many is that?'

'Orbit is a straight deal, Mister Dante. No lying, no bribing. Our customers are "clients", not mooches. Clear?'

'Sure.'

'What makes you want to do phone work again?'

'I wasn't sure until this morning when I saw Frankie Freebase's green Jag convertible. Then I was sure. What time should I be here tomorrow?'

'Our policy is that your first four weeks are probationary. You will be assigned to our "Incubator" on Monday. If you make quota for a month, you're hired. Understood?'

I nodded.

'How many AA meetings are you attending per week?'

'Three, usually. How about you?'

'Three's not enough for someone like you. You've got stinking thinking. Five thirty a.m. Monday morning. Not five thirty-one.'

'I'll be here.'

Kammegian leaned across the big desk. 'Mister Dante, there are three important dates in my life. Would you like to hear what they are?'

'Absolutely. I can't wait.'

'The first one is the date of my birth. The second one is the day I got sober. That day changed my life. And the third most important date in my life is right now! Today. Mister Dante, to hire one champion closer I have to train fifty people. That's the mortality rate at Orbit.'

'You won't be sorry about me.'

'My advice: put your balls on the line. I'm a history buff. Washington is my favorite American general.'

'Glad to hear it. I liked Ronald Reagan.'

'He wasn't a general.'

'He was in the movies. Can I go now?'

'When Washington was outnumbered, outgunned, his army

exhausted and in retreat, someone – a reporter of the day
– asked the great leader if he was considering a surrender.
He hadn't slept in forty-eight hours, he had an unattended
leg wound. Washington looked the man in the eye, never
even pausing. "We shall re-group and attack," he said. You
too, Mister Dante. Regroup. Attack. You have just joined
an elite assault force. And take that ridiculous chip off your
shoulder.'

The big man stood up. His hand was out. 'Welcome to
Orbit. Onward and upward.'

'Banzai,' I said. Then I shook the hand.

Chapter Four

THE MAIN REAL difference between Orbit and the other telemarketing rooms I had worked for in the past was their pitch. That, and that everyone dressed up and wore plastic calligraphy name tags. Eddy Kammegian's script permitted no 'deals' between his salespeople and the mooch – no 'gifts', no 'contests', no color TV's sent to the Office Manager's home address, no all-expense weekends at Trump's on the boardwalk in Atlantic City 'with this next order', no 'rebate checks' mailed to a brother-in-law's address or a P.O. Box.

At my last bucket-shop job in New York selling 'balloons', my office supplies presentation went like this:

Mary-Beth, Dave Conway calling you (you never use your real name when you're selling balloons), Distribution Manager over here at Central Supply. I just got a radio call from one of my drivers. We were making a delivery in your area. Our truck tipped over down the block from you on Fourteenth Street (or Forty-sixth or Seventh Avenue). That's the bad news. Here's the good news: nobody was hurt, and we've got fifty gross of the Paper Mate *look-alikes* with the crates broken open, all over the street. You know these, Mary-Beth, they come in the standard dark blue or black ink. Which color do you use out there, the black or the blue? . . . 'I USE THE BLUE, DAVE . . .' Great! These are the retractables with the silver button on top and the matching pocket clip and they come boxed by the gross ... Mary-Beth, as you know, these normally sell all over town in bulk at 39 cents each but, because of the accident, because my guys have to wrap 'em in rubber bands and stuff 'em into plastic bags, I can let you have these today only at 29 cents a copy. You save $14.40 on each gross. It's a win-win deal for you, Mary-Beth! Now, my question is: Did you want one gross or would the full three gross be better for you? ... 'DAVE, TELL ME HONESTLY; IF I DON'T LIKE THEM, CAN I SEND THEM BACK?' Boy, am I a knucklehead! I forgot to mention about the premium you qualify for just by placing your order today. You're going to be glad I called! Do you like coupons, Mary-Beth? Supermarket double coupons? Let me say it another way: How much do you spend on groceries every week? Fifty dollars? A hundred? Well, enclosed with this order – I'm making a note right now as we speak – I'm sending out $1,000 worth of coupons on everything from detergent to steaks to baked goods to deli coldcuts. Just my way of saying thanks, Mary-Beth ... Mary-Beth, do I need a P.O. or should we just go ahead on your verbal?

That shit.

Now compare the above 'truck tipped over' 'balloon' scam pitching knock-off pens with Eddy Kammegian's Orbit presentation selling legitimate printer ribbons and storage media:

Bob, Bruno Dante calling from Orbit Computer Products. (At Orbit everyone uses their own real name.) Can you hear me okay? ... Great! Bob, are you the one handling the ordering on the computer supplies: the computer ribbons and the re-stuffed laser cartridges? . . . Outstanding. Bob, what my company can do is price protect you. What kind of printers are you folks running out there at Bob's Saddle & Feed? . . . Excellent. How many of those do you go through in an average month? . . . Great. Now Bob, on one gross only of the 4245 printer ribbon at $36.95 per unit, to get you fully price protected on our new high-yield premium product, would the ribbons go out to your attention?

Completely straight. See? His people exaggerated sometimes, but there was no sleaze. Of course, at first, the guy has to object a few times, say he doesn't want any, that he has too many on hand, or that he gets them for less money. Naturally, this is all bullshit. Data Processing guys always lie to get you off the phone. The other thing I found out about data processing guys from working at Orbit is that most of them are inexplicably named Bob.

MOOCH: Okay, sounds great. But I'm real busy right now and I've got way too many ribbons on the shelf. Get back to me in a few months, we'll talk then.

ME: Absolutely. That's no problem, Bob. I know when I call in cold like this you're not going to have an immediate need. But let me ask you a quick question: You *do* have the authority to evaluate on a new product, *right*? I mean, I'm talking to the head and not the feet. *Right*?

MOOCH: Sure, it's my department. I'm the boss.

ME: Great Bob. I don't want to overstock you. You'd lose faith in me, and I'd lose the potential of a good customer. Why don't we do this: I'll cut that quantity in half and go with just 72 only. You can handle that. And I'll put 'em on a slow boat and they won't even arrive until (next week). Oh, and let me give you my name and number just in case you ever need me. Have you got a pen handy?

MOOCH: Right here.

ME: (In this part I give Bob my name and number and make him repeat it back to me. That distracts him nicely. Then . . .) Good. Now Bob, will I need a P.O. on this order, or can I go on just your verbal?

MOOCH: Duh, duh . . . my verbal is okay.

ME: That's an excellent decision, Bob. I'll be getting back to you in a few weeks just to see how well they ran for you. Nice meeting you on the phone.

Chapter Five

JIMMI VALIENTE WAS new at Orbit Computer Products too. Her ass was sensational. Hard. Packed and round like a stuffed foam pillow from Motel 6. 'Masume' was her real name from her mother's side, but she made everybody call her 'Jimmi'. Exotic. Beautiful. Half Mexican, half Iranian. Her desk was located one behind mine in the Incubator, a separate trainee room where all new telemarketers start out. Eddy Kammegian interviewed and hired us both on the same day.

Jimmi was twenty-six, beautiful and street smart, from the Pacoima projects. Completely self-reliant. She had an intense, in-your-face honesty about her. Long black hair and long legs and coffee-with-milk skin and shocking, defiant, blue eyes, and two tiny gold hoop rings piercing the skin of her left nostril. She was six months sober off rock cocaine and alcohol. That first day of our phone training, when we were all introducing ourselves around, Jimmi, like a man would, shook my hand and smiled. When I sat down, I felt my pants. My dick was hard as iron.

She was born and raised in L.A. like me. On the phone or talking to our supervisor, Rick McGee, she spoke perfect television American. But, one-on-one, her dialect was a cross between Van Nuys gang-banger and Twelve Step newcomer.

At the end of day three, the final day of our phone training before our written test, we met after work at Norm's Coffee Shop on Lincoln Boulevard to study and memorize 'The Seven

Keys Of Selling' from Charles Roth's book, *Secrets of Closing Sales*, an Orbit requirement. Jimmi guzzled three Pepsis while I drank coffee. Everything that came out of her mouth was direct and unedited, completely up front.

When we were done with our memorizing, she offered me a ride home in her rag-top bug, then paid for both our drinks while the cash register guy oogled her perfect ass and attempted to make chitchat, wanting to know if he had seen her on TV.

We laughed and talked more on the ride. The back seat of her bug was filled with Barbie Dolls. Sad and old, some with their soiled dresses looking like forgotten hookers in the L.A. soot. Jimmi kept one between her legs as she drove.

When we stopped at a traffic signal, she grabbed her tits and began screaming a crazy imitation of a high school valley-girl brat demanding an implant boob job from her parents. Nuts. Very funny.

Outside my sober-living house in Venice, as I opened her bug's car door to leave, she put a hand on my arm. The blue eyes were like two flamethrowers. She pulled me back. 'So,' she said, already using Orbit's boiler room jargon, '*I am fully price protected! Right?*'

'Right,' I said, playing along, '*Twenty-four months. The total price freeze.*'

Jimmi cooed, 'You were a big help to me today, baby. You know this shit.'

'Hey, any time.'

'You think I'm funny, right? I mean, for a towelhead-wetback bitch?' She grabbed her tits. '*Do these go out to your attention?*'

I had to laugh.

Now the perfect, beautiful smile. A three-finger Pacoima

gang-banger salute against her chest, slipping into vato hip-hop, 'We're da team, esse. Jou know? Iz jou 'n me, homie.'

I copied the salute against my ribs then turned to get out. She held to my shirt. 'What?' I said.

Reaching across me she pulled my door closed. 'I need you to talk to me a minute, man – like real people – okay?'

'Sure.'

She clicked the bug's ignition off, and the motor sputtered dead. 'Gimme a cigarette, okay?'

I handed her the pack.

'Okay, this is like AA, okay? We're both program people. Sober, right? I truss you. Like one alkie talking with another alkie. Okay?'

'Talk,' I said.

Jimmi lit a Lucky and took a deep hit. Then it came out, flooding her bug like a backed-up Van Nuys storm drain. Two years at Santa Monica College studying drama until her drinking and amphetamine habit got out of control. Her amazing looks got her a dozen TV commercials, a full-time Victoria's Closet modeling gig, and a twenty-thousand-dollar check for a nudie spread in *Man's Man*.

Taking another hit, she blew the sweetness at me. 'But see,' she sneered, 'alla tha shit was "BC".'

'BC?' I asked.

'Yeah, you know, before crack.'

It made me laugh.

Her life fell apart. No longer able to hide her drug problem, the disgusted husband, Sean McCarthy, a football player turned TV actor, had given up and moved on. Jimmi got jail time after two arrests in Hollywood for possession. Out on the street again, afraid to deal dope again and violate parole, to support her habit she took up the only gig she could hold: Lap dancing and performing nude at Strip Crazy on Century

Boulevard. During her private session with the johns, she would lean close to ask if they wanted full service. Her blow jobs were two hundred extra.

But, like me, not much had improved in sobriety. 'Attitude problems' caused her to quit or be fired from three dancing jobs in three months. Lately, her older sister's husband, Caesar, had begun demanding that she catch up on back rent or vacate their rear bedroom at the house in Los Feliz. Collection agencies rang her phone in the middle of the night; she had a dresser full of traffic tickets gone to warrant. The pressure of staying clean and working too was making her nuts. Jimmi considered Orbit Computer Products her last shot.

She grabbed my arm. 'Pretty screwed-up, right mijo?' she whispered. 'I mean, lap dancing. Private booths with red curtains. Suckin' dick for money. Tha shit. Thaz deep down even for a loca chola.'

I lit my own cigarette and tossed the match.

There was a connection between us. We both felt it. Two fuckups holding on by our fingers. 'People do what they gotta do,' I said . . . 'I'll help. We'll work together.'

In gratitude, smiling, she ran a long finger over the hair above my ear. 'Right,' she breathed, '"don't quit before the miracle." Right, Bruno?'

'Right.'

But then something was different. She twisted away in her seat. The eyes went empty. 'Hey Bruno, know wha?'

'What?'

'Troof? Okay to say the troof – to say what's up?'

'Okay. Sure.'

'Well . . . don' be mad, but you're like a pussy. You know?'

The words stung. I felt my anger. 'No,' I said. 'I don't know.'

'Before – when we was havin' Pepsis – and right now. You lookin' ah me. All sweet. All fuckin' watery baby-dog eyes n' shit. I mean, you're a pussy. Easy meat. Know wham sayin'?'

I popped the car door open to get out, then turned back. 'You're the one who wanted to talk.'

Leaning across me, she pulled the door closed. Her thick, perfumed hair was in my face – her smell, her tits hard against my arm and chest. Before I could pull away, she was licking my face, my cheek. Two big, wet, slow swipes, the way a friendly Irish Setter would kiss its master. Then she kissed me, deeply. Slowly. Her tongue twisting in my mouth.

Afterward, seeing my eyes and my reaction, she fell back, laughing. 'See? Was I wrong?'

I pulled away, angry.

'If we was in the club,' she hissed, 'you was wit me – private – I could get an extra two hundred, maybe three, no problem.'

'So I'm like a trick, right?'

She giggled, took a new cigarette from my pocket and lit it. 'Done get all mad'n'shit, man. It's jus' the troof. You're easy.'

It was enough. Outside her bug, I put my head back through the window. My mouth wanted revenge. I dug in my pocket, pulling out fifty or sixty cents in change, flinging it on the seat. 'This is all I've got,' I said, tossing the coins at her. 'After we get paid our first checks, I'll have more cash. You can suck me off and lick my asshole then.'

Chapter Six

COLD CALLING IN telemarketing is a weird test of survival. Too confronting for normal people. A hundred calls per shift – face deep in the lion's mouth, hour after hour – dialing for dollars. The bodies pile up fast. By Tuesday afternoon of my first week on the phones, two trainees from our group of four, Jeff Baitz and Prince Johnson, had already quit. Blown out. Jimmi and I were talking again. I knew it was because she was using me, needing my help. We ate lunch together every day. As friends. I didn't care. I liked the company.

But by late Thursday afternoon, she was sinking too. Behind me at her desk, I could hear her slamming her phone down after each cold-call rejection from a receptionist or a data processing manager. Her pitches were monotone; customers were saying 'no' easily after sensing the clumsiness in her typed-out delivery. She had only six deals for the week, four under the minimum limit. Grounds for termination.

On the other hand, I was home, taking no prisoners. After the initial hour or two of uncertainty adjusting to Kammegian's pitch, my old sales adrenaline had taken over. Without cocaine and booze, my head was clear. I was like a dog with a rag in its mouth. I refused to hear 'NO'. I'd cut the quantity, give a dollar off per cartridge as a discount, defer the shipment, propose an eighteen-month price freeze, whatever it took – then CLOSE the deal. My success ratio of pitches to sales was higher than it had ever been. I had twenty-six cold-call deals for the week, tops in the company. Twelve hundred and seventy dollars in solid commissions. Already Frankie Freebase was bragging that he'd discovered the new wonder mouth on the sales floor.

Then, finally, Jimmi bled out. It was Friday morning. She had no deals at all before the break. Sitting together in her car in the parking lot at lunch, I sipped my coffee and watched her chain smoke and drink Pepsis. In boiler rooms, you have it or you don't. '*You buy their tears, or they buy your toner!*'

Furious and sobbing, she grabbed me around the neck. She'd never make quota. She knew it. Today was her last day. All I could say was, 'I'm sorry, Jimmi.' It was then that I realized something: I would do anything to keep her around, help her save her job. Anything at all.

Half an hour later, in the middle of a sale, the solution came to me. A plan. For the next three hours, I dialed my ass off, slamming DP Managers and stock clerk mooches, cutting prices, pushing partial boxes of ribbons, whatever it took. At ten minutes before the last order pick-up of the day, I had six fresh sales in my desk tray. They were small deals, but the size didn't matter. Scooping them out, I erased my own name, then wrote 'Valiente' and Jimmi's Orbit ID number on four of the orders.

I got up to go to the crapper, and on my way passing her desk I slid the pages into her 'out' basket. I knew they would put her at quota and save her job.

After I returned from the bathroom and a smoke, I was at my desk totaling my commissions when I felt the thud of a thick eraser against the collar of my shirt. Behind me the blazing Siamese eyes held nothing back. 'Thanks, babee,' Jimmi cooed. Then, as an afterthought, she grabbed her crotch. 'Wait, vato,' she whispered, 'I suck your dick for free.'

We both laughed.

*   *   *

At five o'clock she was still on the phone, so I decided to go to the bookkeeper's office to ask for an advance. I had won the cold-call bonus for the week: two hundred and fifty dollars.

New Incubator people were normally required to wait an extra seven days to get their first check because of the lag time in verifying orders, but, because I needed the money and because I had won the contest, I'd convinced Frankie Freebase to ask Kammegian for an exception and get me a thousand dollar advance.

It took almost half an hour for me to collect the money. Tilly, the payroll lady, kept ringing Kammegian's line, unwilling to cut me the check and cash it without the boss's personal okay. I didn't mind waiting. I'd had my biggest telemarketing week in years. Twelve-hundred-and-eighty-six dollars for five days work. Take home. No taxes were deducted, because Orbit paid all its phone people as Independent Contractors.

Tilly finally got through to Kammegian and obtained his okay. I signed the pay vouchers. She only had enough money on hand to cash my two hundred and fifty dollar bonus, so I was given a payroll check for the rest.

I was leaving Payroll when Doc Franklin walked in. Orbit's top salesman. We hadn't met yet, but I had heard about him from Frankie. My supervisor, with a sneer, let me know that Doc would be easy to recognize. His trademark at work was his crazy hats. The man behind me in line sported a thousand dollar business suit topped off by a leather WWI aviator's helmet, complete with a beanie propeller.

Tilly introduced us. Franklin's smile was ear to ear. Honest and friendly, not filled with grease like Kammegian and Frankie Freebase.

Doc put his thumb and pinkie finger to the side of his

head pantomiming a telephone, '*Do these ribbons go out to your attention?*'

I played the game, snarling, '*Bob, I am fully price protected!*'

'First two weeks, right?'

'Right. First week on the phone,' I said.

Playfully, Doc snatched my pay vouchers from my hand. After seeing the amounts, he thrust his palm in the air to be high-fived. I slapped skin. 'My man!' he roared. 'Only one week on that horn! Almost fifteen hundred bucks! Twenty-six new accounts! Outstanding!'

'Thanks,' I said. 'Feels good.'

'You're sober too, right?'

An odd question. 'Four months,' I said. 'Why? Does it show?'

Doc laughed, then reached up to give his helmet propeller a spin. 'Just a guess. Around here, we're all ex-juicers, junkies, and crack heads. I figured you for a member of the club.'

I smiled back. 'I've joined an AA cult, right?'

'More like a sober success machine. Around here, it's white flags or toe tags. Eddy calls it, "sur-fuckin'-render"!'

Tilly handed Doc his sealed pay envelope. After signing the voucher he tore the flap open, then passed the check to me. He hadn't looked at the amount inside. I read the numbers in disbelief: $7,099. One week's commissions.

I handed it back. 'Hey,' I said laughing, reaching out to check the amount again, playing the sales pitch game, 'that really is *the price protection.*'

Franklin shook my hand. 'Keep it up, my man! You're on your way. Orbit's a million dollar deal. Problem is, we shove it up your ass fifty cents at a time.'

We laughed.

*   *   *

When I got back to the Incubator, Jimmi was gone. The room was deserted, the lights out. I was about to leave when something drew me to her desk. A queer need to be where she had been, to be intimate, to feel her presence.

Looking around to make sure I was alone, I pulled her chair out and sat down. Jimmi's heat, her perfume, the pulse of her, was everywhere. I could feel her.

On the desk pad next to her computer was her office stuff: a freshly washed coffee mug, a row of sharpened pencils, a calculator, a scratch pad, paper clips, brochures to be envelope-stuffed and mailed out, and a stack of order blanks. A Barbie Doll in a Harley Davidson outfit rested against her phone. Everything was neat, ready for the morning. I began touching and handling each thing, wanting to experience what she experienced.

The Incubator door hissed open. Toxic Bob, another trainee, came in. I stayed motionless in the semi-darkness. Without looking around or turning on the overhead lights, he went to his desk, grabbed his jacket off the back of a chair, then left the room.

Alone again, my fingers found one of Jimmi's pencils, a short one. I handled it, then wrote my name on a scrap of paper, then rolled the wooden-ribbed sides against my lips. The same fingers that had written with this pencil had also visited the magic place between her legs. I licked the yellow covering until its salty taste was gone.

Pulling open her top drawer, I continued my tour. At first, there wasn't much: a pack of Kleenex and more office paraphernalia, a cheap stapler, erasers, paper clips, a glue stick, a lined box of 3x5 cards, and two Baby Ruth candy bars. But lifting the cards, I discovered a small treasure: Jimmi's lipstick. The dark red that touched her mouth. Sacred.

Sliding the gold tip off I drew a thick line on my tongue.

The taste filled me, shocking my mouth. Jimmi's taste. Wondrous. Intense.

I was seized by a perversion. For a moment, before acting, I listened for footsteps in the hall. There were none. Then, unzipping my fly, I pulled out my cock. Taking my time, I painted the head of my dick with the gooey red stick. With each smudge my cock got thicker, more swollen. The fear that another late Incubator straggler might re-enter the room intensified the trip.

Lowering my pants to the floor, I began to jerk off. Long, slow strokes. In less than a minute, I felt myself ready to cum. Grabbing the closest thing – Jimmi's Pepsi mug – I let go my load. Blast after blast, into the cup.

When I was done I found the pack of tissues and wiped my cock, then pulled up my pants.

Stealing her lipstick was a petty thing to do, but I had to have it. It was hers. A relic. Clicking the top back on, I dropped the tube into my pocket, then left the room.

Chapter Seven

THE NIGHT CLEAN-UP guys were wheeling in their maintenance cart as I was leaving. It was five thirty. Orbit's parking lot was empty. I'd missed my ride with Frankie Freebase, but I didn't mind. If I wanted to, I could take a cab home or call a limo service in the phone book or stroll over to Santa Monica Boulevard and write a check for a down payment on a cheap used car. I had enough money to do whatever I wanted.

Sitting on the Lincoln Boulevard bus bench, smoking Lucky cigarettes, I began to think about Doc Franklin and his amazing paycheck. My brain swarmed with monthly and yearly income projections. Doc was knocking down over three hundred grand a year. If he could do it, I could do it too.

I came to an immediate decision: fuck my writing career. My head was clear for the first time in years. I could foresee my own future. Novelists and screenwriters like Jonathan Dante died broke in L.A., humiliated, compromised. Their balls and their talent sacrificed to a ridiculous Hollywood success fantasy. No one cared about words any more. Literature was deader than a *Seinfeld* rerun. Seventy percent of Americans now got all their opinions and information packaged, formatted, spoon-fed through a three-foot square marketing box. The preposterous dream world created eighty years before in Los Angeles between the sand and the planted palm trees and the tumbleweeds, Sam Goldwyn's and B.P. Schulberg's and Mayer's and Karl Lemmle's image of America, was now the national mindset. A nation of mooches. Writers were dinosaurs. Chumps. Real life was a cop show and a pair of silicone tits. So what.

A noise interrupted my mindtrip. The jolt of a honking horn. Looking up, I saw Jimmi's dented, sputtering, rag-top bug at the curb five feet in front of me, her smile whiter than a priest's collar. 'Hey, homie white boy,' she laughed. *'Got a fuckin' pen handy?* Wake up and get in, fo some vato motherfucker mugs your sleepy pendejo telemarketing ass.'

I felt the blood go to my face. Walking to the curb, I got in. Before pulling out into traffic, she leaned across the seat and kissed me. Not a long kiss, no tongue this time, but a sincere kiss. A good kiss. A Barbie in its pink dress was between her legs. 'Thanks for today, Bruno,' she sang. 'You saved my ass.'

I smiled. 'I did it for me, not for you,' I said.

We drove to Orbit's bank, so I could cash my pay check before six o'clock. Her driving was more homicidal than before. Aiming at pedestrians, weaving in and out between cars, screaming at the other drivers. She yammered on about Rick McGee, our Incubator supervisor: He'd called her into his office to congratulate her on making quota and pump her up, even promising to give her special help and coaching.

Leaving Washington Mutual Bank on Lincoln Boulevard, my pants pocket was stuffed with bills – hundreds and twenties and tens. Back in her bug, I suggested that we drive to Venice Beach. I wanted to celebrate by buying us dinner at the Sidewalk Cafe. Jimmi aimed her VW in the direction of Rose Avenue, then stomped the gas pedal.

The heat of the day had faded, and the breeze off the Pacific had a dry, sweet, taste. We got lucky and found a parking space half a block from the sand. She threw her Barbie in the back seat, and I took my tie off. We left our shoes in the car.

On the boardwalk at the Sidewalk Cafe, I spent fifty bucks on salads and pizza and two chocolate ice cream pastries shaped like Elvis. Laughing and talking. I told her about the poetry I'd published, leaving out that I hadn't had anything in print in years. When our waiter came to collect for the bill, I did a version of the Orbit sales pitch on the guy, trying to *price protect* him on giving up his tip. Walking away from the restaurant, Jimmi kissed me again. A long, hard, tongue kiss.

Next door at Small World Books, I stuck my head in and asked if they had any Jonathan Dante titles. The lady behind the register looked at me. 'Jonathan who?' she said.

At an outdoor stand, I bought us cigarettes and cappuccinos, and we began walking the strand. Men we would pass looked back at Jimmi, their eyes aching. She ignored it, sucking her cappuccino, happy to hold my arm. Playful.

We stopped to look at the beach vendor stuff: the jewelry tables, tee shirts, knick-knack and souvenirs stands, the tattoo artists and fortune tellers. Jimmi bargained with the Latino ped-dlers, shouting negotiations in Spanglish. Her smile changed everything – she had them cold. While she was talking to a jewelry guy, I palmed a hundred dollar bill and handed it to his sales clerk for a beaded silver necklace in a gift box.

In half an hour, we had two shopping bags full of junk; knock-off perfumes, literature from the Hari Krishna's, sun glasses with exchangeable lenses, stuffed Disney toys for her nieces I had never heard about, a cigarette lighter shaped like a skull, a twelve-pack of cold Pepsi, a cheap watch, ten kinds of incense. Crazy shit. And two gold pillows with the words 'VENICE BEACH' sewn across the front.

With me towing the bags, Jimmi pulled me by the arm the width of the wide beach to a place near the surf where we could be alone. Flopping back in the sand, she pulled her skirt up above her hips revealing long, brown, strong legs. At the top I could see a pair of silky black panties. The sight of them made me choke.

'Pussy brain,' she snapped, when she saw me staring. 'Hey Bruno, *you got a fuckin' pen handy?* Stick your eyes back in your face, man. You seen legs before.'

'Not those. *Those are the premium. The high-yield. The extra life.*'

'You can't see my bush, can you?'

'No.'

Licking her fingers, she reached over and shoved them into my mouth. 'Guys! Always thinkin' wich yo dicks. Don' chu know tha makes a women feel all creepy'n shit?'

'Then pull your dress down,' I said, sucking the fingers. 'Stop flashing *Your shipping address* . . . Are the underpants silk?'

'How 'bout I pull 'em down so you can see my monkey; how 'bout tha shit, mister telemarketer, mister literary genius richass fifteen-hundred-dollar a week success phone guy?'

I laughed. 'You're making my tongue hard.'

'Hey Bruno, chill. Fow I buss a cap in your white-boy ass.'

I pulled the felt box containing the silver necklace out of my jacket pocket and put it in her hand. 'Okay,' I said, 'I've got a surprise.'

While my heart thumped, Jimmi bent the lid open to look inside. She smiled when she saw the gleaming trinket with its inlaid black stones. She took it out of the box and held it up. 'Jesus, mijo,' she whispered, sliding toward me across the sand; 'thaz beautiful.'

Then, a second later, her face was dark. Changed. She handed the box back.

'What's wrong?' I asked. My stomach had gone hollow.

'I can't take tha from you, man.'

I searched the stained-glass eyes. 'Okay, why?'

'You know why, man. You bought me nice stuff today,' she whispered, 'Fun stuff. But this don't mean tha, this means somethin' different. I know how jou think, man, okay? Jou thinkin' it's you'n me. Tha ain gonna happen, Bruno. You and me ain in love, okay?'

I should have waited, filled my mouth with a handful of sand or seaweed before talking, but I didn't. 'So, you're a mind reader,' I snarled. 'A psychic. Madam Jimmi from the Pacoima sewer. Because I bought you a piece of fucking jewelry, now I'm going to ask you to marry me. Is that it?'

'Baby-boy,' Jimmi whispered, touching my arm, her nails teasing my skin, 'I like you. Jou my man. Jus forget the flowers'n shit, okay? Jou'n me ain down wid tha.'

I jerked away. 'You're right. Fuck it!'

'Chill man. I tole you – you'n me ain tha way.'

While she looked on, I got up and flung the necklace as far as I could into the surf.

'Yo, man! Why'djou do tha?'

'It's mine, that's why! I bought it and paid for it with the money I made working, closing MY sales. If I feel like feeding the fucking sharks, it's my business.'

She was on her feet spinning in the direction of the boardwalk. 'How'bout this, bitch; *you* suck *my* dick. Okay!?'

Then she was gone.

Ten minutes later, the sky had gone dark red. Still carrying the shopping bags, I made my way back across the sand and down the boardwalk to where we had parked the car. Jimmi was waiting there, smoking a cigarette, sitting on the front fender of her bug. Walking up, I dropped the bags at her feet. 'These are yours,' I said.

She opened the car door, then stuffed the bags inside on the floor. She handed me my shoes from the front seat. I could tell she wanted to make up. 'Clean your feet off before you get in,' she whispered. 'Please. Okay?'

Leaning against the car, I slid my socks on then pushed my feet into my loafers. 'Fuck it,' I said. 'I'm walking home.'

'C'mon man, be nice. Get in the car.'

But I hadn't had enough. I peeled a twenty dollar bill off the wad from my pocket and thrust it toward her. 'Here,' I spit. 'Gas money. Thanks for the ride.'

She pushed the bill away.

Turning away from the beach, I began walking toward Pacific Avenue. Then something caught my eye – stopped me. Several cars away, up the block, a fat, grey-shirted meter maid was forcing a parking ticket under the wiper on a jeep's windshield. Looking over at Jimmi's bug's window, I saw she had one too.

I felt my anger. Stepping to her car I yanked the pink cardboard envelope out from under the wiper then read the inked-in handwriting: 'OBSTRUCTING HANDICAPPED ZONE – $237.00.' Jimmi's car's front bumper was a foot or two into the blue area – sloppy parking – but clearly obstructing nothing. 'Hey you, ticket bitch!' I yelled up the block, unable to stop my mouth.

The meter maid heard me but didn't look up. Fifty feet away she was occupying herself writing an expired-meter summons.

'Hey,' I yelled louder, losing control, waving the cardboard ticket over my head. 'Hey, parking cunt! What in the motherfucking goddamn fuck is this!'

Jimmi was beside me, clutching and grabbing to hold me back. But it was too late.

The uniformed woman was tall, over six feet, a heavy-framed black lady. As I stomped in her direction, she thrust her arm out, her flattened palm toward me, in a cop-like 'stop' gesture.

'Hey yourself,' she barked, tossing her ticket book on the roof of a ten-year-old Camaro, 'hold it right there!'

I kept coming. 'This is bullshit!' I yelled. 'Two hundred and thirty-seven dollars worth of handicapped, blue-curb, bullshit!'

Reaching her, halting inches from her face, I tore the ticket in half, then in half again, then tossed it against her huge tits. 'How 'bout that, fatasspigparkingfucker? Half cop piece of shit, half fuckin' gofor civil-service, Gestapo parkingmeterfuckingcocksucker! . . . Fuck you! How about that?'

The big lady leaned forward. We were chest to chest.

I shoved back – hard – losing my fists in her tits.

'Mister,' she snarled, 'that's assault! You just impeded the duties of a City of Los Angeles Parking Enforcement employee. Now you got you some real trouble.'

Pulling a two-way cop radio from her belt, she punched the broadcast button. 'This is P-V-B-217. I've got a problem here. Come back?'

Jimmi's eyes showed her panic. With the strength of a man, she yanked me away by my shirt, then steered me five feet in the opposite direction. 'Bruno, Jesus! Stop it, man.'

I wrenched myself free.

'Quit!' she pleaded. 'I told you I've got a drawer full of tickets and Failures To Appears at home. Man, they run my plates, I go to the fuckin' slam!'

Sidestepping me, she swiveled and came face to face with the meter maid. 'Sorry for the problem, Miss Officer,' Jimmi begged. 'My friend's an asshole. You know, from New York.'

The big woman's walkie-talkie was still to her mouth. 'That

man just assaulted a municipal employee,' she barked. 'There's back-up on the way.'

Jimmi was in my face, yelling. 'Gimme your money!' she hissed. 'All of it!'

Reluctantly, I dug in my pocket for the wad. She grabbed the bills then, whirling, facing the woman, she peeled off three hundreds and handed them across.

The meter maid clicked her radio off. 'What's this?' she demanded, a thick arm holding up the money. 'Now you attempting to bribe a civil employee?'

Jimmi handed her another hundred. 'Lady, I don't *need* any trouble. Please understand?'

The woman eyed her coldly then stuffed the money into her pants pocket. 'Girl,' she snarled, 'you'd bess watch yo man. He got hizzelf a bad mouth and some real ugly manners.'

Huffing, with effort, she bent to the sidewalk, scooping up the fragments of the torn parking ticket, then tucked the pieces in her pocket with the money. For the first time she was smiling. 'We gonna forget all this ever happened.'

Five minutes later, back in her bug, Jimmi popped a Pepsi, then lit a cigarette. 'Jou like a two-year-old brat, mijo.'

'Four hundred fucking dollars! Are you joking?'

Instead of answering, impulsively, she kissed me. Passionate. A long kiss. Her sweet, squirming tongue filling my mouth. When she was done, she opened her eyes and drew back, her hand on my leg. 'Jou in love wit me, right? I know it so don lie, man.'

Taking a chance, I moved her hand across to my crotch. Her smile was playful. She flung the Barbie between her legs into the back seat.

The red sky had turned mostly black, but it was too early for stars. Another kiss. Long, hard, and deep. When she was done she unzipped my fly. My dick was iron.

Afterward, we were both smoking, staring into the impeccable night. 'Feel better now?' she whispered.

'Exceptional.'

Then her hand was between her own legs, rubbing her spot. 'I want that cock inside me, Bruno,' she breathed. 'Can I tell you what else I want, what makes my twat wet?'

'A necklace. Jewelry?'

'I want you fucking me while that fat-parking-bitch watches us. Like she's standing on the sidewalk with her fucking ticket book in her hand looking in the window. Rubbing her cunt while she's talking on her cop radio, reporting us. Your cock is everywhere in my body. And she's watching you lick me. Then you cum again, and I suck every drop and spit it out all over my tits . . . Is what I'm saying making your dick hard, Bruno?'

'Jesus!'

Laughing, another deep kiss, her tongue squirming – probing. Her hand was back in my pants, stroking my dick.

'You're good at this,' I whispered.

Jimmi laughed. 'Two older brothers, mijo. I should be. I been sucking dick since I was seven.'

Wetting two long fingers in her mouth, she reached down between her thighs. As she did, I felt her tremble. 'Right now. Okay? Fuck my cunt. Fuck me right now!'

Pulling the fingers up I watched as she held them to her mouth then licked. Then she forced them between my lips. 'You hear me, Bruno, I want you in my cunt, now!'

She was on me, straddling me in the passenger seat. Black sweet-smelling hair wet against my face, her powerful hips like a battering ram, fucking my dick like a death monster.

Chapter Eight

OVER MY TWO weeks at Orbit, I'd gotten Eddy Kammegian's personal history in bits and pieces through Frankie and some of the other sales guys. The company's president was a born again symbol of success. He had sobered up after five years of being a hopeless, homeless, juice head and coke hype. While still in a residential recovery program, Kammegian found phone sales by accident as a temp job. For him, it was like hitting the lotto. After only six months on the phone selling computer ribbon, he managed to 'close' an uncle who owned grocery stores on lending him the seed money to open his own supply business. *One call turns it around.* Orbit Computer Products was an instant success. After that came self-help and sales courses: The Forum, Tony Robbins, Og Mandino, Brian Tracy, Zig Ziglar, Tommy Hopkins.

Eddy staffed his small telemarketing business by rolling up to AA meetings and alkie recovery homes in a white, leased, four-door Benz; passing out pockets-full of business cards, pitching the barely-dry newcomers on sharing the dream.

Jimmi's attitude toward me was different since the weekend. I assumed the change had come because of the meter maid incident and the money. We'd had sex again. Only once, but it was good sex. For her own reasons, she had stopped allowing me to kiss her. We would eat lunch together every day in her bug, parked a dozen blocks from Orbit on a side street near Santa Monica Airport, smoking cigarettes and talking.

My Chrysler Fifth Avenue was repaired and purring like a kitten. Three hundred and fifty horses humming on all eight cylinders. Cuco, the Panamanian guy down the block who did moonlight mechanical work out of his two-car alley garage, got it running good. Cuco's hourly labor, a rebuilt battery and boiled-out junkyard replacement carburetor and spark plugs cost me just under four hundred dollars. It was a good investment, because I was sick of standing in the cold, before dawn, listening to Frankie Freebase's nut-job rantings.

My AA sponsor, Liquor Store Dave, made sure my nights were filled with Alcoholics Anonymous obligations. Like a goosestepping robot, on instruction, I would leave work promptly at four p.m. to pick him up. After that, we would have dinner at Norm's or Denny's on Lincoln Boulevard with a couple of the other guys he sponsored, then we would all go to an AA meeting. When it was over, again following Dave's orders, me and the other guys would pass out our phone numbers to the newcomers, then help sweep up. I still didn't like AA much. All the smiles and hugging and over-worked cliché's and bad coffee hadn't made me feel any more comfortable. There are Twelve Steps to do in the Alcoholics Anonymous Program. Liquor Store Dave told me I was still on Step Number One.

I had just celebrated five months sober, and a couple of weeks had passed since I had had any desire to drink; even so, not sleeping remained a major deal. No matter how tired my body was, at night in my dorm in the recovery house, my mind refused to shut itself down, hour after hour regurgitating and resifting preposterous, infinitesimal shit. Sometimes there would be waves of panic, crazy ununderstood fear about losing my job or losing Jimmi. My mind rehearsed all our conversations in advance, careful to conceal the depth of my feelings, the intensity of my need for her. Eventually, exhausted, I would find myself downstairs in the community kitchen with Jonathan Dante's old portable typewriter, doors closed to contain the sound, writing unpunctuated, rambling poems and crazy letters that I would never mail. Page after page of the shit would come out until I had tired myself enough to go back up to my room and fall asleep.

Two weeks later, at five thirty on a Friday, I stayed late at work, waiting in line for my regular commission check. Jimmi was still on the telephone selling. Because it was pay day I had negotiated permission with Liquor Store Dave to take the night off from AA. My plan was for Jimmi and me to have dinner at the Mexican restaurant at the top of the Huntley Hotel on Second Street in Santa Monica, then get a hotel room until midnight, my curfew time at the sober-living house. I wanted something expensive with a view of the ocean.

After picking up my check, I came back to the Incubator to discover she was gone. Loomis, one of the guys in her row, was the only employee left in the room. I asked if he knew where she was. Snickering, he pointed a finger in the direction of our supervisor, Rick McGee's office. The door was closed.

I felt a stab in my stomach. Like being knifed. It was hard to inhale. 'You didn't know, my man,' Loomis sneered, 'your pal, hot little Ms Valiente with the Barbie Dolls, is McGee's pet project.' Then he grabbed his crotch. 'You know, *pet*, as in pet-da-pussy?'

'Since when?'

'All this week, man. After work. Ya dig?'

'You're saying you saw them?'

'*Hey Dante, I'm giving you the fucking two gross price here.* My desk faces McGee's office. You go home at four o'clock. I stay late, so does Miss Valiente. And here comes tall-ass McGee ... I see her go in there after work for half an hour, an hour sometimes, ya know, then come out. Every day. *You* tell me what they're doin'.'

'It's none of my business,' I said. 'Valiente can hump the Boniventure Hotel for all I care.'

'Yeah?' jeered Loomis, 'tell that to your face, man.'

I hated him. I wanted to yank the cheap ball-point pen from his shirt pocket, then jab the fucker into the eye socket behind his nerd-shit eyeglasses. Instead, I walked away, back to my old desk, pretending to be checking to see if I had any phone messages.

I had to know for myself.

I hung around until Loomis went home. Then I shut the Incubator lights off and moved to another desk with a better angle view of McGee's office, keeping my eyes fixed on the line of light beneath his door, holding the phone to my ear, ready to fake a conversation in case they came out. Soon, thinking it through, I realized Loomis was right. I felt it. I was a fool. God had found a way to fuck me again. I mocked myself and cursed my heart. She had stopped letting me kiss her. I should have known then. This woman sucked cock the way most people say 'hi' in an elevator. I hated her for the whore she was.

Disgusted and shamed, seeing the truth and my stupid obsession, I got up and moved toward McGee's door. I was about to slam it with my fist when cowardice – like the smell of something dead – stopped me. The thought of seeing her with McGee made me freeze. Turning my back, a whipped dog, I walked out of the Incubator.

In the break room, I smoked a cigarette, stalling, guzzling stale coffee, thumbing through magazines. I had to see her. There was no purpose to it, just crazy, addicted need. It didn't matter that a hundred feet away she was probably on her knees licking McGee's cum off her lips.

Three stragglers from Doc Franklin's sales team, waiting for their pay checks to be printed and signed, came in and poured coffee. Having fun. Joking. They hardly noticed me with shame and self-disgust oozing from my pores.

One of the girls, whose name badge read 'Sylvie', recognized me and said 'hi'. Pretty. Outgoing. We'd met before. A week prior in the copy room. Sylvie had been impressed by how quickly I had caught on to Orbit's telemarketing program. She'd even congratulated me on winning my first cold-call bonus. Then we'd had a ludicrous conversation where I had pretended to be grateful for the compliment and acted as if I were interested in how she was doing. As if I gave a fuck.

She stood above me. Smiling. Making conversation. She wanted to know what team I would be on when I left the Incubator. I couldn't answer. I looked up into her eyes, but I couldn't talk. My mouth began twitching. A mute dufus, I half tried to form a word shape, but nothing came out. Finally, I lurched to my feet, then left the room. All I cared about – my single intelligible thought – was McGee's office.

I decided to wait for Jimmi in the parking lot, watching the exit until she left the building. No one would bother me there.

Walking down the hall past the payroll office, the glass door suddenly swung open. It was Jimmi, her check envelope in her hand. A young male employee was holding the door, watching her pass, leering at her ass. Then, a second later, McGee came out too.

Seeing me, uncomfortable but trying to act pleased, she shuffled up. 'Yo mijo,' she whispered, 'where you been? I've been looking for you.'

She pulled me a few feet down the corridor and gave me

a long hug. 'I found out I'm okay,' she hummed. 'My orders went through and got verified. I made quota again. I got my check.'

Face to face with her, I was wet bread. 'Look,' I said, fumbling for my two Orbit checks, pointing at the numbers, grinning like an idiot, 'I'm rich. Over two grand. Let's drive to the beach. We'll have dinner.'

Her smile was a wonder. The eyes, two flawless blazing blue beads. 'Sorry, baby,' she whispered, pulling me closer, 'I can't. I'm staying. Rick's been helping me, coaching me with my pitch. We're going to get a bite, then go back to his office.'

She was lying, and I knew it. My anger hissed like spit. 'It's Friday night, Jimmi,' I snarled. 'Almost six o'clock, Friday-fucking-night.'

'Man, shhhh! Keep your voice down. He's helping me. He wants to work late. Okay?'

'Hey, what about this, I'll come too. I need his fucking "help" too.'

'I said no, Bruno. Okay? I tol'jou, man. I'm busy.'

I was yelling now. 'How fucking stupid do you think I am?! You're sucking McGee's dick!'

'Mind jour bizniz, motherfucker!'

I was out of control, but I couldn't stop. 'Answer this then: while you're fucking him, do you whisper that you want it up the ass!!? Do you beg him to cum in your mouth?'

She stepped back. 'I said shut your face, man!'

'Did you lick his asshole?'

She tried to edge herself down the hall in the direction of the ladies room, but I grabbed her arm. Screaming, she pulled back, but I held on.

The commotion brought tall McGee rumbling down the

corridor. 'Let her go, Dante,' he demanded, cuffing me from behind. 'Let the woman go. Right now!'

Freeing one hand, I shoved him off. 'Tell the truth, asshole! I want to know! Are you fucking my whore?'

'Last time, Dante. Let go!'

'Lick my scrotum, gerbil shitbrain!'

McGee's punches came in rapid succession. By the time the throbbing started, I was sitting on the floor with my back against the hallway wall, holding my nose, blood and snot dripping down on my shirt from between my fingers.

Chapter Nine

THE MONDAY MORNING following the trouble, I was drinking coffee, taking a break, demonstrating a quick close technique to my new teammate, Neil. A move I had learned while selling porno movies. It works like this: The mooch says, 'Look, I don't need any videos (or light bulbs or gizmos) right now. I've got a year's supply in my storage room.' Acting surprised, the salesman says, 'Look Bob, I would *never* want to overstock you. But let me ask you this: it's *your* department, you're the boss, right?'

The quick close works eight out of ten times. I mean, what's the mooch going to say to that kind of question – 'No, I'm a lackey, I only clean the toilets here.'

Out of the corner of my eye, I watched Frankie Freebase come down the stairs from a meeting in Kammegian's office. He walked directly to my cubicle, then motioned for Neil to go back to his own desk. 'You're wanted upstairs in the boss's office,' he said, spitting the words. 'Now!'

'Okay. What for?'

'Well, dicko, let's just say that Kammegian ain't invitin' you up there to present you with a new Chevy SUV. Get goin'.'

I slid my chair back and stood up.

Frankie was leering. 'You didn't tell me what happened outside Payroll last Friday. Now, you're fucked.'

'It was an argument. Nothing. It wasn't important.'

'Swell. Try running that down on Kammegian. By the time

you get back here to your desk, I'll have your shit packed up and you'll be ready to rejoin that sparkling-fucking, unique-fucking, thrilling-fucking team of cocksuckers selling vacuum cleaners and home maintenance crap where you worked before. You're history at this company, asshole!'

I had tried to call Jimmi all weekend. Once an hour. Twenty or thirty times. I kept getting her answering machine. I knew the locations of all the AA meetings she attended: the one at Twenty-sixth and Broadway in Santa Monica on Saturday night and the other one on Sunday at twelve thirty on Ohio Avenue. She hadn't showed up at either place. I had even driven by her house, but her car was not in her sister's driveway or parked on the street. All weekend I had stayed in my dormitory room near the hall pay phone, smoking cigarettes and trying to read. Waiting. She never called back.

The owner of Orbit Computer Products was on the telephone at his PC when I knocked and came in. I let the door hiss closed behind me. Looking up, Kammegian motioned me to a chair.

Behind him at eye level on the Orbit Trophy Wall of Champions was an imposing World War II photograph of Winston Churchill. I hadn't noticed the picture at my job interview, because it was blocked by his big leather chair. General George Patton was up there on the wall too. His photograph was even bigger than Churchill's. And Colin Powell. And Norman Schwarzkopf. All part of my boss's military armed-forces-self-improvement obsession. When I leaned close to the desk, I was able to make out the engraving on the brass plate below Churchill's image. It read: 'Never give up – Never, never give up.'

Kammegian ended his phone call, then rolled back behind the center section of his desk. 'Okay Mister Dante,' he said, 'let's hear your version of what happened at the Payroll Department on Friday afternoon.'

'My version is – I picked up my biggest paycheck yet.'

My reply induced a smirk. He rocked forward and let his elbows come to rest on the desk pad. 'Exactly. First things first. Right?'

'One day at a time,' I chimed back.

Kammegian stood up and extended his hand. 'I would like to personally recognize you for your outstanding work last week,' he said. 'Winning the cold-call bonus again was an impressive accomplishment. Over two thousand dollars in commissions for five days work. Right?'

I shook his hand. 'Right. All solid deals. Everything verified.'

We both sat down.

While I watched, my boss resituated a paperweight by his telephone, rocked back again in his big chair, then tucked his legs back under the desk.

Withdrawing a custom-imprinted pencil from a shiny metal holder by his Rolodex, he began toying with it, running his manicured finger over the lettering on each side, then pricking his thumb with the point. I was starting to relax when, suddenly, in a kind of fit-outburst, my boss slammed the spine of the fucker straight down at his desk. Yellow fragments detonated and flew everywhere. A good-sized chunk zinged past my cheek.

'Equivocation is disloyalty, Mister Dante! You're full of shit, and your two-thousand-dollar-a-week job is on the line here this morning. Let me caution you, I have zero tolerance for what took place on Friday afternoon. So, let's back up. What happened in the Payroll Department?'

'You mean outside Payroll?'

'Do not fuck with me, Mister Dante.'

'Okay look,' I said, brushing remnants of pencil shit off my sleeve, 'the whole deal was a misunderstanding. A miscommunication.'

Kammegian rocked backward. 'Explain your version.'

'I lost my temper.'

'And – what happened when you lost your temper? Did that contribute to further *miscommunication*?'

'Okay, I made a remark. Several remarks.'

'I see. And you made these remarks to another trainee or to a supervisory person?'

'To Jimmi Valiente. And to McGee too.'

'That's what you're calling a *miscommunication*?'

'Essentially. Basically. In a nutshell.'

'Then – *basically* – the reports I have, one from another sales person and one from Tilly Hickman in Payroll, about a fist fight by two of my employees, are both incorrect? More *miscommunication*?'

'Tilly was in her office, and the other person, whoever that nosy, lying cockfuck is, was not in the hall either. In my experience, Mister Kammegian, my opinion: most people, out of some snotass ego need to make themselves appear okay in their dismal, chicken-shit, insect, ratshit, little lives, are prone to make presumptions about matters they don't know thing-fucking-one about. There were only three people in that hall: me, Jimmi Valiente, and McGee.'

Kammegian selected another pencil. This one's point was sharpened too, but the stem was longer; brand new, right out of the box. 'Last time, Mister Dante: were you involved in a fight or not?'

I knew he had me. 'Okay, I was,' I said, 'but it wasn't actually a fight.'

'Explain *actually*, Mister Dante.'

'What I mean is, it wasn't technically a fight in the way you mean. McGee shoved me. To me, literally, in concept, a fight is where one person physically, actually, slugs the other person. That didn't happen.'

'I see. So we're talking about a shove here, not a slug. What about the bruise on the side of your face?'

'Completely unrelated. I'm coming clean here, Mister Kammegian. One recovering alkie talking to another. I banged my face on the metal paper towel dispenser at the 76 Gas Station on Lincoln Boulevard on Saturday morning while gassing up my Chrysler. No big deal.'

Eddy Kammegian was on his feet. He paced around the side of his desk, then sat on the thick mahogany edge facing me, his shiny belt buckle eighteen inches from my nose. When he crossed his arms I could see his shirt cuffs were fastened by two gold Civil War cannon cufflinks. Fat diamond studs glistened from where the caisson spoke wheels should be. 'So it was no big deal?'

'Right,' said I. 'My injury isn't work related. Therefore, no big deal.'

'Is Ebola no big deal, Mister Dante? A virulent epidemic that could easily bring a company or a city or an entire army to its knees?'

'Somebody at Orbit has Ebola?'

'Last time, asshole! You, me, Rick McGee, Ms Valiente. We're all eating out of the same pot. Orbit Computer Products is a finely-tuned elite assault machine. Any employee disturbance, any dissension, spreads through our sales organization like a toxic virus.'

'Hey!' I said, 'I understand. Like a turd floating in Orbit's steaming vat of delicious tomato soup.'

Kammegian reached around and yanked his telephone out of its cradle. Before dialing, he turned back to me: 'How many sales did you make this morning?'

'Two so far.'

'I'll have Tilly cut you a final check.'

I was on my feet. 'Wait!' I yelled, 'Jesus, I'm cooperating! I told you what happened.'

'Sit down, Dante.'

I sat down.

'Have you been "involved" with Jimmi Valiente? The truth, please.'

'We became friends.'

'YES or NO?'

'We had dinner together. We hung out.'

'And McGee? What about him? Is Ms Valiente "friends" with Mister McGee as well? Was that the problem?'

'Ask McGee. Ask her. I'm not involved with Jimmi. There was no fight.'

'There are three words I want you to consider before you leave my office today: procrastination, deception, and masturbation. They are the best ways I know that a man can fuck himself. I hope you get my meaning.'

'Check.'

My boss crossed the room and opened his office door. 'Meeting concluded.'

'I'm not fired?'

'Have you been candid and one hundred percent forthcoming with me this morning?'

'I want to keep my job, Mister Kammegian. I like my job.'

'Then go back to work. Have your manager locate Rick McGee and send him to my office. Do that now.'

'Okay,' I said, walking away. 'Thanks.'

'Onward and upward, Mister Dante.'

My boss spent the rest of his day conducting interrogations.

His secretary, Elaine, was up and down his office steps twenty times, a yellow legal tablet tucked under her arm. Jimmi and McGee were called in. And a guy in the parking lot that afternoon who had seen me with my face bleeding as I left work, Bowen Kessler.

The next morning, Tuesday, I was writing up an order when Kammegian's secretary tapped me on the arm then stuck a 'Post-It' note by my telephone. The Post-It read, '8.17 a.m. You're wanted in Mr Kammegian's office.'

Upstairs, my boss was waiting, hands folded on the desk in front of him. 'Sit down, Dante,' he snapped.

I did what he said. But as I did, he lurched to his feet, then paced to the bay window overlooking the sales floor. He began flipping the blind open and closed by pulling its strings one at a time. An imitation of Field Marshall Rommel pondering a Panzer deployment.

Nervous, knowing something bad was coming, my eyes came to rest on the shiny pencil holder by his desk. The supply had been replenished.

Finally, he abandoned the window to walk around behind my chair. I could feel him there, his hands on the backrest near my neck. 'Does the name Todd B. Baskin mean anything to you?' he half hissed. 'Has Frankie Freebase ever mentioned that person?'

'No.'

'This spring, Dante, a low snake coward saboteur named Todd Bennington Baskin betrayed me, violated his fiduciary responsibility to Orbit Computer Products, and was arrested for theft. Baskin was once a highly-respected commando at Orbit Computer Products. My V.P. of Marketing with an income of over 200k per year. My left hand.

'*Left* hand?'

'My higher power, the God I've come to know and experience

through the program of Alcoholics Anonymous, is my right hand. Baskin was my left hand.'

'Okay. Right.'

'Question, Dante: Why would a man, a highly successful, trusted man, a man with a 2,200 square foot condo in Beverly Hills and partnerships in three shopping centers, a man with an honorable discharge from the United States Navy, risk everything, his entire career and his freedom, over a petty obsession? Can you answer that?'

'I have no idea. Was he a wine drinker?'

'Baskin burgled his reorder account books and several vital account history CD's from these premises in an attempt to open his own computer supplies operation: a felony. Of course, his attempt failed and he was apprehended.'

'And I hope the jerk got what was coming to him.'

'May I continue?'

'Go ahead.'

'A staff sales person who was working late the night of the crime witnessed Baskin skulking around outside in the parking lot, then smuggling a box of company files into the trunk of his car. The act was later verified by our exterior surveillance video camera. The point, Dante, is that someone stepped forward. That person knew Baskin; they were friends actually, but his loyalty to Orbit Computer Products exceeded his personal concerns.'

'Great. Crackerjack.'

'Stand up, please.'

I stood up.

Kammegian was in front of me. He started to say something then paused a moment – the death pause – then he handed me an envelope.

'What's this?' I asked.

'Open it.'

Inside was a payroll check for three hundred and eleven dollars along with a pink form paperclipped to the top. The form read NOTICE OF TERMINATION. I tried to hand it back. 'I want another chance,' I said.

'You've been writing front-call orders for Ms Valiente. You've been fucking her. Both you and McGee. You erased your own name on your sales orders, then filled in her I.D. number.'

'I'm in love with her.'

'You're fired. Get out of my office.'

Chapter Ten

YOU SLEEP.

Sometimes, in a panic, you wake up in the middle of the night, not knowing where you are. Bolt upright. After you realize you're okay, you suck back a half-dozen pulls from the bottle on the floor by the bed. You smoke a cigarette. Two. If you've had enough whiskey, you can fall back to sleep. Sometimes.

In the morning you come to and start puking. But you must drink again right away to hold off the heebie-jeebies. So you drink and you puke some more, because the booze won't stay down.

You try eating food to settle yourself. Anything. Stale bread. Dry cereal. Peanut butter by the spoon. Anything.

Eventually the food stays in your stomach, and you're okay and you can start again. The best thing, of course, is vodka in orange juice. Or ginger ale. Cold. Cold is always best. If you haven't got vodka, a beer. But it has to be cold. If it's not cold, you'll puke again. And that's how it goes – if you have money. If you've got money, you've got no worries – not a care in the world.

Sometimes my runs lasted ten days. Two weeks. How long they go on depends on how much my body can take. When your ankles and feet stay numb all day, it's time to ease off.

The day I started back, I had a fistful of hundred dollar bills, clean socks and underwear in my drawer, and a 5.00 p.m dentist appointment for an examination because my gums bleed all the time. I was thinking constantly about Jimmi, but I had made no conscious decision to drink again or even had any thoughts about it. The morning after Kammegian fired me, I was up early, slurping coffee in the communal breakfast room at my recovery house, re-reading my story, 'Compatibility'. I remember for once liking what I had written. Straight up fiction. Dashiell Hammett. Boom boom short sentences. Like my father's stuff. Hemingway. My twenty-five pages were just right for the high-end man's magazine market. I had made up my mind to send the story off.

My plan for that day, except for the dentist, was to completely re-read my story, attend the movies, and go to an AA meeting with Liquor Store Dave. Because money was no problem, I told myself that I'd start looking for a new telemarketing gig in a week or so.

After more coffee, upstairs at the hall payphone, unable to stop myself, I dialed her number again and again. I wanted to say I was sorry and say hello.

Jimmi's sister, Sema, with the two kids, answered the phone. One of them was crying in the background. Sis said Jimmi was in the bathroom and asked me to hold on. There was yelling through the door – Jimmi shouting something back. Sema asked me my name. I told her, 'Bruno'. Jimmi yelled something in Mexican, then the phone clicked dead.

On my way to the movies, I stopped at the 7–11 for cigarettes. A guy was sitting against the wall outside the store – a street guy. Shaking one out. He wanted chump change for some beer. We talked for a minute.

Thinking back, that was how it started. I bought him two

cans of Coor's and brought them out. I didn't drink with him, but my mind did. I never let go of the impulse.

Parking my Chrysler at the movies, I was twenty minutes early. I hate the fuckasshole commercials and trailers and the hard-sell stuff they make you watch for fifteen minutes before the feature, so, with 'Compatability' under my arm, I walked to the bookstore nearby to kill some time, to see if they stocked any titles by the dead writer, Jonathan Dante.

The bookstore was closed. The sign in the window said opening time was one o'clock (the same time as the movie). Next door was an air conditioned sports bar: the Alibi Room. I walked in. Not a second thought – no hesitation at all – found a stool, set 'Compatibility' down on the bar, then ordered a double Stoli shooter with a beer back. One sip and I was home.

An hour later, Cin walked in. It was the beginning of the second inning of a Mets/Dodgers game on TV. I had finished re-reading my story about a dating service salesman being seduced by the red-haired manager of a uniform store.

Cin was short for Cynthia. Australian with an accent. Lovely large floppy tits. Her friend with the big hair and the shopping bag was Nikki. Cin had been in America for twenty years. She was older than me by a dozen years, but pretty. Short blonde hair. Ass wide and ample. By comparison, Nikki's ass was huge, a hippopotamus ass.

Cin ordered tequila and smiled at me when they sat down. Nikki ordered something red that came with an umbrella.

Piazza homered early with two guys on, so the game was in good shape. The girls were talking about their vacation in Barcelona. They were animators at The Kartoon Factory in El Segundo.

Mike, the barkeep, was coming and going behind the bar. He and the weekend bartender, Stu, were involved playing a video game. Yelling and whooping and high-fiving in an imitation of a commercial for basketball shoes. When any of us at the bar required another drink, we had to contend with getting Mike's attention.

Closest to me was Cin, only a stool between us. Nikki had anchored her ass on the far side. Everything Cin said was in a low voice, a semi-whisper, which I liked. Sexy. I learned from the girls that animating is a lucrative occupation. It's piece work, but when animators are being paid to animate, the money is excellent. The two of them traveled a lot together and made excursions to various foreign destinations.

My buzz was good and my money was on the bar: a stack of hundreds and twenties to impress the girls. I was paying for their drinks and for mine, but Mike clearly didn't give a fuck about his patrons because of the video game. I tried tipping him ten dollars, but it didn't help.

'Compatibility' was in front of me. I said I was celebrating a film deal. Big Nikki suggested that she and I might have friends in common at the studios and wanted to know who I was doing business with. What producer. What production company. I changed the subject.

The Dodgers got five runs in the third and two in the fourth. I bought us each three rounds, so we didn't have to worry about Mike. Presently, good and drunk, I began to put a move on Cin. I told her 'Cynthia' was my favorite woman's name. My aunt's name was Cynthia. As a kid, my family had pet bull terriers, brother and sister, named Rocco and Cynthia.

There was a sweetness about her. Not like the insanity in Jimmi's eyes. A gentleness from some old sadness. She knew New York too. Manhattan and Soho and the upper West Side, The Ansonia Hotel. While we talked, she leaned over to pick a piece of lint off the front of my Yankees cap.

Mike came back and poured more drinks then switched the

satellite station from the Mets to hockey without asking shit from anybody.

Soon, big Nikki was bored and drunk. Five tiny, bent, pink umbrella sticks spelled out 'N I K I' on the bar. Finishing her drink, she suggested to Cin that they both should leave. After some conversation I didn't hear and a quick phone call from the cell portable in her purse, Nikki went off alone.

Cin and me continued talking. It turned out she was an avid reader. Agatha Christie and that stuff, but Harry Crews and Sherwood Anderson too. And Herman Hesse. Even one or two by Selby. Her breath was sweet, and her thighs were firm and strong against the inside of her thin dress. She was touchy too, putting her hand on my arm as we talked. She asked if she could read 'Compatibility' and wanted me to loan it to her. I shook my head no. My last copy, I said. It was my only copy.

One drink later, she leaned close to my ear. 'Time to go, Bruno,' she whispered. 'Meeting friends for dinner.' Then she kissed the side of my head. 'You're quite drunk. You should go too.'

The sadness in her was deep. It filled the room and touched me. Impulsively, carried away by the emotions of the moment, I passed her my story. 'Okay,' I said, 'read it and send it back.' I wrote my Venice P.O. box number and zip code on the front by my name. Then I said, 'Can I tell you something?'

Cin was smiling. 'Of course.'

I leaned close and put my hand on her leg. 'The way your body looks in that dress makes my dick hard.'

Her eyes came alive and began to twinkle. She tilted her head back. 'Say that again.'

I kissed her neck. 'I said, you make my dick hard.'

Her fingers were on my arm. 'You have to look at me when you talk.'

'Why? Are you a lip reader?'

Without shame she pulled the hair back on the left side of her face. There was no ear where an ear should be, only an indentation and a smooth scar. 'I have to be face to face when we talk.'

'You're deaf?'

She nodded, looking almost afraid. 'I hear a bit out of my right ear, but not much,' she whispered. 'So, say it again, Bruno. I am interested.'

Being sure she saw my mouth, my words came out too loud. 'I love you. Could we go somewhere and fuck?'

Cin laughed. 'Not today, angel.'

'When?'

'Would you like my phone number?'

'I would. Yes. I want your phone number.'

Taking a pen and a business card from her purse, on the back she wrote her name and a Hollywood 323 area code number. The penmanship was perfect. 'Drive safe,' she said. Then she was gone. 'Compatibility' under her arm, a sweet melancholy lingering behind like the quietness of jasmine.

Now it was only me and Mike. Stu, his video game partner, was gone. Walking back from the pisser, I stopped by Ninja Bloodbath/Marauders of Death. A kickboxing video deal. Mike was still at the machine. I watched for a minute. It was bullshit. A preposterous child's amusement. The principle of the game appeared to be maiming your opponent by karate kicking, then hacking and dismemberment. There were controls: two red buttons and a joy stick.

He sensed me behind him, and I knew it made him uncomfortable. I didn't care if Mike was uncomfortable. Mike was an asshole, a crime against the environment.

I continued to watch the action. His warrior was getting nailed and sliced up. The opponent, the computer, was piling up points. Then Mike settled down. He pounded the buttons in front of him, wiggled furiously on the joy stick, and made his guy leap in an impossible twirling pirouette. Down he came, hacking off his opponent's fighting arm. The next move was a gore to the throat. A nifty one-two. The tide had turned. Mike's digitized killer began bouncing up and down waving his weapons, waiting for the opposition to get up. Oozing blood and bodily fluids, the enemy squirmed in an attempt to get to his feet. But Mike tapped crazily at his red button and his man showed no mercy, kicking out viciously with a stiletto-pointed armored boot. Down again went the opponent, the spike driven deep into his forehead.

It was time for the game's final move. Mike's killer did a flip and crashed down on the fallen warrior's skull. Blood and brain tissue squirted against the inside of the video screen. Death! Victory! 940,000 points.

'How 'bout it, Ace,' Mike sneered. 'Wanna play? You and me.' He was ready. His neck veins throbbing. 'Tell you what,' he said, 'I'll make it easy; ten bucks a match. Loser buys the drinks.'

'How about fifty bucks a game?' my mouth shot back. 'How about that, *Ace*?'

'You know Bloodbath? You play?'

'Fifty bucks a game,' I said. 'Here's mine.' I slapped a hundred up on the glass.

After he had won the first round, we began going double or nothing. Half an hour later, I was cleaned out. Twelve hundred dollars.

I was evicted. That night at the recovery home, Chickenbone, the manager, saw me come in drunk. That was that. While I was packing I kept trying to call Jimmi from the upstairs payphone but her sister's answering machine kept clicking on, screening my calls. After a pocketful of quarters, I finally left a message. '*Jimmi – Bruno . . . I'm moving out. Tonight. They kicked me out . . . You there? I'm sorry you got fired. I got fired too. I want to see you. I want us to talk.*'

I heard a click, like someone was listening on the line. Then it went dead.

Chapter Eleven

MY RUN LASTED nine days. Drunk around the clock with the blinds down and porn movies blinking at me from the TV. My new home was Room 117 at The Prince Carlos, a U-shaped, fifties-style 'remodeled' motel on Sepulveda Boulevard. Before the neighborhood changed the building had once been two floors of furnished studio apartments. Now it was $197 per week. Two weeks up front. The Carlos was the only motel on the street advertising air conditioning, weekly rates, and all rooms with HBO and Adult Movies. 'Se habla español.'

It took several days for the crazies to start. It had been over half a year since the last time, but now they were on me. It was bad. I had been sleeping only an hour or two at a stretch and hadn't got drunk enough – hadn't been numb enough – so when I fell asleep there they were – the terrors – the phantom fuckers. Huge bastards, scurrying around, the size of dogs – bodies like roaches – on my wall, scooting along, their lizard fucking tails twisting, up the ceiling and across, one side of the room to the other. Watching me as they crawled. Leering. If I woke up with a jerk, sat up, sometimes it would take a full minute or two for the images to go away.

Sometimes I would hear them in the drawers. Or the floor creaking. They bred in closets, hidden places. By the hundreds. Scratching noises everywhere.

A day later, with a lot more booze, it got better because I

kept myself awake, burning myself on the arm with the tip of my cigarette.

Scratching. Scratching. Scratching.

If I had to piss, I pissed in an empty vodka bottle, pissed over everything because I was shaking. Pissed on my fingers. On the sheets.

Then finally, exhausted, I slept.

When I opened my eyes, it was to a different noise. Outside, the rumbling sound of the motel maid's heavy, metal-wheeled cleaning cart. I realized it must be morning. I had no idea what day. My body hurt. I couldn't move. My face, my legs, my back. Pain everywhere.

Looking around, I saw that I was not in my bed. I was in the bathtub, naked. With me was my stuff, all that I owned: shoes, bottles, clothes, my typewriter, a fake plant, a suitcase, my books. I had relocated my life to the bathroom. The sharp pain at my temple was being caused by the volume dial of my portable radio.

Shifting positions, I looked at my watch. Seven o'clock. On the linoleum floor was a bottle. Half empty. I took a long hit. With the drink came an acute awareness. I was now fully crazy. If I kept going, I would be dead.

I was hungry. My shakes were bad, and the sourness in my stomach was choking me. I unloaded the tub, slowly, one object at a time, then moved all my shit back to the main room.

After puking, I took a slow hot shower, putting down the rest of the vodka; then I found a shirt and got dressed.

In the daylight on the staircase of the Prince Carlos Motel, it took a long time for my eyes to adjust. When I had convinced myself there was nothing crawling near my feet, it became okay to walk across the asphalt to my car.

I drove slowly to Vons market and purchased cold beers to

taper down. A ham and cheese sandwich from the deli section. Only one quart of vodka.

Back in the Chrysler, after I ate and drank two beers, I felt okay. Better. I still had the shakes, but I congratulated myself on making it out into the world. I decided to drive to the beach to my Venice P.O. box. I hit the radio. The blues station. 88.1. Otis Redding. 'I Been Lovin' You Too Long.' I cranked the music up to make sure it was louder than my head.

At the post office, opening my P.O. box, ten days of congested pulp spilled out. There was a big brown envelope. Even before I looked to see who it was from, I knew the sender was the sad Australian woman. Then I saw the handwriting, formal, calligraphic. My returned manuscript. '*Cynthia Appleton. 8743 Wonderland Avenue, Los Angeles, California 90048.*' Postmarked two days before. Safe to open.

Most all the other stuff was crap, but two letters worried me. One had a New York law firm as the return address; I assumed it was my ex-wife's attorney. Another one, an evil-looking, blue-bordered prick, note size, bore one of my mother's stick-on return address labels. The postmark was a week old. Trouble. I threw everything into a trash bin except Cynthia's package and mom's note.

I was right.

Mom's letter was to notify me that my brother, Rick, was dead from an exploded ulcer. Forty-eight years old. The family genius. Jonathan Dante's first-born pride and joy. Ricardo Frederico Dante. Rick Dante. My big brother. Chess champion at ten, scholarship to art school, one of the designers for NASA of the flexible struts that held the first space stations together. A thinker. A guy deeply into books and Wagner and the histories of weird SS German generals. A confused, sad, isolated, bad-tempered, damaged mooch of a guy. Dead from years of scouring his large intestine with two quarts of whiskey a day. First Pop, then Fat Willie. Now Rick. Dantes were dropping like flys.

I shoved mom's note down into my pants pocket, then locked my P.O. box.

Outside, at the top of the steps, I was hit by a blast of summer heat and dizziness, so I sat down. The mighty Pacific sun had worked its way above the buildings, blinding me. A dozen nearby roofs had become shimmering, punishing, mosks: vengeful fire gods reflecting their contempt on anything not young and tan and imbued with L.A.'s frenzied TV optimism.

Below me were people, locals coming and going around the Venice Boulevard traffic circle. Skateboarders. Mothers pushing strollers. Rollerbladers. People attending to the business of Monday. Lighting a Lucky, I took a deep hit and leaned back out of the glitter. Soon the day would be swarming. Pizza stands and ten-dollar parking lots would fill with tourists and immigrants talking in thirty different languages. Another perfect, cloudless summer day in the endless California dream. And my brother Rick was dead. Insignificant by comparison. Nothing at all.

A girl in a tight two-piece bathing suit skipped by me up the steps into the post office, her thighs brown and flawless. A depilatory commercial.

I opened Cynthia's envelope. Clipped to the cover of 'Compatibility' was a note on Victorian-looking pink paper telling me how much she liked the story. Little fat angels with roses in their mouths floated along the paper's border. Cin's telephone number was there too.

The post office has pay phones in front, so I punched in the number and let it ring.

I had forgotten Cynthia was deaf. When she answered, her

voice had a distant, officious tone. She asked me to speak up and told me that an amplification gadget was attached to her earpiece.

I immediately realized that the call was a mistake. I was unprepared for conversation. My brain began pounding. Cin started asking questions, normal conversation shit. Too much. How was I? Was I writing?

'I'm sweating,' I said. 'My brother Rick is dead. How are you?'

Speaking his name triggered a phantom. Suddenly Richard Dante's sour face was in my mind: a sneering, twisted genie. Part hangover, part insanity from my motel room. It felt like the asshole was standing next to me on the concrete – in my face the way he used to be when we were kids.

I began shaking.

Attempting to save myself I hung up the telephone. But I could smell this ghost's odious, stinking breath. To quell the stink I lit a new Lucky Strike, took a deep hit, and sat back down on the concrete.

In a few minutes I was calmer, alone again.

In my pocket I found more quarters, got up, and re-dialed Cin.

'Bruno, you rang off.'

'AT&T. The fucking telephone company. The Military-Industrial Complex.'

'. . . Much better. I can hear you quite clearly now. Did you say someone died?'

'You said you liked "Compatibility"?'

'You have a great imagination. Have you written other things, more stories, more screenplays?'

'I lied about the film script, Cin. I've never written a screenplay.' *(There he was – again – suddenly. Next to me. Less form than voice this time. About twenty years old, hissing* in my ear . . . 'Wait! Ha-ha, my brother, a writer?' he ridiculed. 'When did that happen? Is this some kind of idiotic, witless, preposterous attempt at humor?')

I was shaking again. Dizzy.

('Who is this twat? I know! This is the thick-thighed fat-ass blonde from the bar? That Australian bitch?')

'Bruno, you have to speak up. I can't hear you.'

'I'm not really a writer.' ('Whaddya know, the truth! Our father was the writer, a giant of words, a poet, a raconteur. Tell her that. What you are is a regurgitating, moron fuck. A pathetic outpatient.')

'What, Bruno . . . I'm sorry.'

I was dizzy, passing out. I had to hold on to the frame of the phone stand to keep myself upright. 'Cin, I have to call you back.'

'. . . Why? What's wrong?'

'I'm a telemarketer . . . An unemployed boiler room phone guy. I'm not a writer. Not really.'

('Thanks for the honesty, bitch! What you are is a loser. A Twelve-Step recovery-home cripple. Now tell this deaf kooze about the twelve hundred dollars you lost gambling at that fucking video game. Tell her, cheese dick!')

'Please don't hang up. "Compatibility" is your story? It's a good story. You wrote it, correct?'

My body was breathing hard, sucking air in and out, half-coughing words into the phone. 'Let's get together for a drink, Cin. I want to see you.' ('Drink? What drink? You want pussy. Say it! Pussy, pussy, pussy. You can smell the tangy stink of her snatch right here over the phone. Tell her that.')

'Please slow down. I'm losing what you're saying.'

I formed the words carefully. 'I want you to ask me over to your house. Can we get together?' ('Now it comes! The begging! Shit-pants little Bruno.')

'That's sweet.'

'Is today okay?'

'You sound . . . a bit odd, Bruno. Are you alright?'

'I said my brother's dead . . . I just found out.' *('What happens when you're in the sack with this fat kooze and you decide you want a blow job? Think about it! What do you do, use fuckin' sign language?')*

'I'm terribly sorry, Bruno.'

'Cin . . . I like you. I like watching your eyes move while you read my lips. I need to talk. To be with someone. Do you mind?' *('Fuck you! You don't give a rat's dick about my rotting body. You want pussy!')*

'I've got appointments and errands to run until this afternoon.'

'I remember Cin, you like tequila. I'll pick some up on my way. Okay?'

'About three? I'll be home at three.'

'I want to kiss you, Cin.'

'You're very impulsive.'

'You want to kiss me too – don't you?' *('I'm about to shit myself here . . .')*

'. . . Okay. But Bruno, only to talk. I'm quite serious. I don't like moving fast when I first meet someone. Please understand.'

'I know your address. Laurel Canyon, right?'

'I'll see you at three.' *('Outstanding, dickless! You have the verbal acuity of a Central Avenue crack dealer.')*

There was a homeless guy at the bottom of the post office steps. Young and drunk. In his twenties. Toothless gaps when he talked. Seeing me smoking, he waved his hand, pointing at my Lucky cigarette.

I handed him one. When he saw what it was – that it had

no filter – he tossed it over his shoulder into the street. 'Got anything else?' he cracked. 'I smoke filters.'

Cin's house on stilts and her big red cat named Camus had come in a divorce. Gerald, the ex-husband, was an important corporate guy in the London/L.A. music business. Nineteen years into the marriage, one night at dinner over a bottle of Pouille Fousse, Gerry let Cin know that he took it up the ass. He'd decided to go full-time gay with his Puerto Rican lover, Ugo. Along with the house and Camus and a permanent case of the empties in the divvy up, Cin got four thousand a month in alimony.

It took me two hours, a shower, a Burger King Whopper and half the quart of Stoli, and blasting my car radio, to quiet my brother Rick's voice. My Chrysler was running good except for a funny engine smell, and the A/C was blowing cold. I took Venice Boulevard east toward downtown L.A. When I got to La Cienega, I turned left to Pico, then over at Crescent Heights. Crescent Heights turns into Laurel Canyon Boulevard when you get into the Hollywood Hills.

Chapter Twelve

CYNTHIA'S HOUSE WAS two miles up Laurel Canyon in the hills. On stilts. Wonderland Avenue. The back of the place, the garage, was against the road on the land side, and the front deck extended out over the canyon's sheer wall. In L.A., the term for that is 'cantilevered'. From inside, at an angle, when I looked out below, I could see the long poles that anchored the bottom of the place to the side of the hill. Then – a hundred foot drop – straight down. My mind reported to me that any minute the whole deal would give way and cascade my ass to the bottom of the gully. In the old days in Hollywood – the 40s and 50s – according to my father, Jonathan Dante, who worked as a contract screenwriter at Columbia and MGM during those years, Laurel Canyon was where all the brothels were located. Gambling and hookers. Many nights, rather than drive north on the Coast Highway to Malibu, Pop would shack up and play poker in Hollywood at The Garden of Allah Hotel at the mouth of the canyon on the L.A. side. Nat West. Scott Fitzgerald. A.I. Bizzarades. Bud Schulberg. Faulkner. Willie Saroyan – all came and went at The Garden of Allah.

There were two copies of my story 'Compatibility' on her piano. One was mine, and the other one was a Xerox duplicate Cynthia had made for herself on the copy machine in her den/office. She had all the gadgets an animator needs to work at home – an oversized computer, a printer, a fax machine, even a scanner.

Cin's hearing aid was on, and we drank more tequila sunrises and sat outside reading my story to each other while Camus the cat lolled between us alternately demanding affection, then displaying fat indifference.

By the end, on page twenty-five, the place where the guy selling the dating service leaves and never comes back, Cin was drunk and had tears in her eyes. She put her hand on top of mine. 'Wonderful,' she whispered.

'Thanks,' said I.

'You're better than Raymond Carver.'

'Raymond who?'

She handed me a pen. 'Autograph it, please. Inscribe the following: "To Cynthia: In appreciation of our new and wonderful friendship." Then sign it, "Your devoted, Bruno."'

It was my first autograph of anything, to anybody. I dumped fat Camus off the couch and was about to write on the cover when Rick Dante's voice began clanging in my head, louder now: *('Hey pussy, wait! Write this: "I will do anything for a piece of ass." Then sign it, "Love always, Approval-drooling Twatbrain."')*

'What's wrong?' Cin wanted to know, her thousand-year-old eyes watching my lips.

I handed the pen back. 'It's *devoted*,' I said. '*Devoted* is excessive.'

'One day *The New Yorker* or *L. A. Magazine* will publish this story. You'll be famous, and all I'll have are these scraps of paper.'

'I'll never be famous.'

'I want to commemorate this afternoon. Is that so fucking *excessive*?'

Camus the cat was waddling toward a corduroy chair in the living room. I pointed at him. 'That's *devoted*,' I said.

She handed me back the pen. I finished my drink then wrote, 'For Cynthia, devoted *best wishes. Bruno Dante.*'

She read the inscription then grinned. 'Splendid. Date it too.'

I did, then looked around in my head for Rick Dante. He was gone.

'You're the Shake-fuckin'-speare of West Hollywood,' Cin slurred. 'You're Tennyson. John-fucking-Fowles.'

'I'm Stan Laurel . . . Will you suck my dick?'

Cynthia laughed. 'Absolutely.'

For thirty years I'd had the dream off and on. After Cin fell asleep I eventually dozed off and had it again that night: at Saint Monica's Grammar School when I was eleven, mean-assed Sister Sirenus caught me and Paul Foley in the back of the room fooling around, having fun at the expense of weird Rudy Espinoza.

Sister had ordered Espinoza up front by the blackboard to give the answer to a history question. On his way up our row Paul chanted, 'Rudy, Rudy why so fruity?' Hearing it, I chimed in. The class laughed.

Espinoza was a simple kid, a fact that was common knowledge to all including Sister Sirenus who liked to use him when she felt the need to illustrate how stupid American students were as compared to the more precocious Catholic-educated kids in the Ireland school system where she grew up.

As usual, Rudy had been daydreaming and blew the history answer and was given five demerits. Everybody laughed. Once again SS had demonstrated how stupid and miserably feebleminded us American kids were.

He marched back past me to his desk.

It was then that I made the mistake of getting caught making a jerk-off gesture – pounding my doubled fist against the crotch of my school-blue slacks. More class laughter. SS saw me do it, and then saw Paul Foley imitating my hand movement.

She squelched the room's sniggering by loudly slapping her pointer against the top of her desk. She had not traveled seven thousand miles to be saddled with a room full of hypnotized, drooling buffoons – dim-witted, mannerless hooligans. She slapped the desk again and again with her ruler. Our fifth grade class had just born witness to the commission of mortal sin. Full stop. This was no laughing matter.

Justice was swift for me and Foley. Our lesson was humility. The room was deadly silent as he was ordered up front and given six whacks across his open palms – three on each hand. Zing, zing, zing!! . . . Zing, zing, zing!! And twenty-five demerits; the most any of us could remember one kid getting, all at one time.

I got twelve whacks – six on each hand. Then Sister let the class know that she was reserving the full measure of my penance until after school. She needed time to confer with her Lord and Savior.

At five exactly, I waited alone, scared shitless, in the cold classroom for Sister Sirenus. It was getting dark, and the ticking of the wall's ancient clock continued to remind me that I was missing the last bus back up the Coast Highway to Malibu.

Sister Sirenus shuffled in in her black Zorro getup half an hour later. I kept my eyes on the linoleum, but I could sense the fury of saved-up convent rage. Did I know *precisely* what I had done?

I nodded.

Was I aware of the seriousness, the evil, of the hand gesture I had used in her classroom that day? Did I know what that hand gesture really meant?

I nodded again.

I could feel SS's face getting redder. Did I know that every time a boy like me committed the sin of masturbation, it was the same as murdering *one* baby. God saw everything. God was watching me right now. Did I know that me and every other boy who masturbated was no different than Adolph Hitler? Did I know what abortion was?

I shook my head. I wasn't sure what abortion was.

Sister wrote it on the blackboard in big capital letters; 'A B O R T I O N', then snapped her chalk, drawing a thick line beneath the word.

Masturbation was a form of abortion. Murdering the unborn was called abortion. The corpses of the babies I had murdered would gnaw the flesh from my skin for all eternity in the fires of damnation. Sister wanted a note from my mother verifying that I had told her precisely what I'd done. Sister wanted it on her desk by the following morning. I was to go to confession on Saturday, inform Father Burbage of my sin, using the word 'masturbation' in a complete sentence, and ask for his and God's forgiveness.

It was over thirty years later. Satan and I had become old buddies, but I still hated the fucking dream.

In the morning, she was gone while I stayed in bed. Off to submit a portfolio full of sketches for a walking toothpaste tube to some guy at Paramount TV. A big, sad woman with wonderful fat tits. So needy. Wanting somebody to replace the vanished husband and fill the hole in her heart that she could not fill herself. Her paintings and sketches were full of it; the house was full of it. Emptiness.

There was no tequila left in the kitchen, so I switched to scotch with my coffee and ate microwaved English tea cakes in bed. An hour later, I realized I had overdone the scotch when I started making phone calls to Jimmi's sister's number. Hitting the re-dial button again and again. Hanging up when her machine came on.

My room at the Prince Carlos was paid for the next five days and I had plenty of money in my pants, so, feeling good about what Cynthia said about my story, I decided to try some more writing.

On my way back to the motel, still drunk on the Australian girl's scotch, I pulled into a big liquor store deal on Robertson Boulevard to stock up. Benny J.'s Wine & Spirit Mart.

The place had everything: a toy aisle, greeting cards, even a vitamin section. I bought a carton of Lucky cigarettes, three quarts of vodka, cranberry juice, orange juice, and cold cuts and mayonnaise for my motel room's little fridge, beer, several jars of cashews for breaks and watching TV, a jigsaw puzzle, and a pack of 100-sheet, 20-lb erasable typing bond. The excursion took an hour. Up and down the lanes, pushing a red plastic cart.

When it came my turn in the check-out line, the clerk eyed me and made a face. He seemed to disapprove of the slow way I was unloading my purchases on to his conveyor belt. A gay kid, college age, impatient. American Philippine, with a ring through his pierced eyebrow and dyed white blond hair and barbed-wire tattoos around each wrist. His name tag read, 'Todd – Assistant Manager'. I grabbed two tabloids off a rack and tossed them on the moving counter.

'Will that be all?'

I nodded 'yes' but threw on two king-size Snickers bars from a candy display.

'Sir, will that be all?'

'Yes Todd, that will be all.' Then I changed my mind and

tossed on an additional pack of Life Savers and a pouch of Red Man chewing tobacco. Impulse purchases.

'Cash or charge, sir?'

I peeled off a hundred and put it on top of the rolling twelve-pack of beer. 'Cash, Todd.'

As he was feeding my stuff through the register's scanner he hesitated while swiping the peanut jars. 'Sir, the sale is on the beer nuts only. The Benny's Beer Nuts.'

'I don't eat beer nuts. I don't like the skins.'

Todd huffed and rolled his eyes. 'Okayyyy – sooo . . . which jars of nuts do you want, sir?'

They all looked the same to me. 'The cashews,' I said. 'I only eat cashews. I don't care about the sale.'

'Sooo, no Benny's Beer Nuts?'

'Correct. No Benny's Beer Nuts.'

'What about the Benny's Mixed Nuts, sir?'

'What about 'em?'

'You have two jars of Benny's Mixed Nuts here. I assume you can read, sir?'

'A selection error. I don't eat Benny's Mixed Nuts.'

Todd snorted, shook his head, and made a conspiratorial 'what-an-asshole' face to the guy behind me in line. A construction guy with two cases of beer in his cart, wearing a sweaty *Nobody Knows I'm Elvis*' T-shirt. 'Great sir,' sneered Todd, making a dramatic deal out of sweeping the extra peanut jars aside.

Behind me Elvis snickered. The woman behind him with fleshy arms shook her head. This was Todd's turf. Making customers eat shit was a skill he'd refined. 'Sooo then,' he hissed, 'you don't want the Benny's Mixed Nuts and the Benny's Beer Nuts even though *you* are the one who put them in your shopping cart?'

More chuckles and snickers.

Me and Todd were face to face separated by the moving conveyor belt. 'For the last time, Todd, I only eat Benny's-fucking-Cashews.'

'Sir, I just asked a question. A simple question.'

'Can I ask you a question, Todd?'

'What is it, sir? I'm waiting. And, as you can see, everybody behind you in line is waiting too. Our store is extremely busy this afternoon, but *you* have a question. What is your question, sir?'

I could feel myself losing control. I leaned across the counter. 'Are you a cocksucker, Todd?'

'Excuse me?'

'It's *just* a question! I'll ask it again: Are you a motherfucking faggot cocksucker?'

Todd stepped back, and so did the other customers. This was L.A. A 9mm automatic pistol might accompany my outburst.

But I was done. I grabbed my money off the register, then tore the tab up and away from one of the cans of Benny's Mixed Nuts, emptying the container on the counter on top of the jigsaw puzzle and the other shit.

Out in the parking lot, after I got in my Chrysler and put the key into the ignition, I noticed something strange: I had an erection.

Chapter Thirteen

I TRIED TO write, but I couldn't. Nothing came out. I would scribble a sentence, then sit there and forget and write it again. I attempted to rework some poems. Nonsense. Guff. As a solution I turned on HBO and continued with vodka the rest of that day and into the night. Then, for an hour, I walked, attempting to tire myself. I slept a little, woke up, and started on the booze again.

But something had happened. I had lost the ability to get drunk. It had been replaced by a black, bottomless depression. My body was slow and unresponsive, but my mind stayed lucid, yakking away, wanting to kill me. Finally, I figured out what it was. The cause. It was Jimmi. Thinking about her, I had made myself impervious to alcohol. The time I had spent with Cynthia, her irreversible sadness, had only made Jimmi's presence more profound. I could smell the smell, close my eyes and see her, feel her next to me on my bed.

It was morning. I got up, vomited, and drank again. Still haunted by these thoughts, I opened my legal pad, and sat at the desk. If I couldn't write anything worthwhile, I would write to her. So this is what I wrote; '*Jimmi*' it began, '*I walked last night. I couldn't sleep, so I started walking south on Sepulveda Boulevard in the direction of the airport. The whole time it was about you. Stupid miscommunications and problems. I mean this: it's all my fault. Not yours. I'm the fool. I overreacted. I'm sorry.*

I passed by a darkened Methodist church, a crazy place at three o'clock in the morning. A ghostly place. I realized that I might have lost you for good. I sat there and tried to pray. But, as a kid, the nuns told us that Methodists and Jehovah Witnesses and Jews and everybody else who is not baptized in the rapture of Jesus is lost. All damned. Crazy, diabolical, Catholicism. These people must convert to the true faith or burn forever. So I knew the prayers didn't work. Then I had the thought that maybe I'm not really a Catholic. The idea came to me; I might have been switched at birth for a fucking Seventh Day Adventist or a Baptist. Anyway, without you, I'm doomed too, Jimmi. Empty. A goddamn fool. Please call me. Bruno.'

It was a preposterous and childish letter. I tore it to shreds and threw it away.

To keep myself from going crazy, I decided to go out and copy my story. I didn't care if I got stopped for drunkenness. Locked away. I wanted to be arrested. I deserved it. I was alone now. The woman I cared about was out of my life for good. Like a madman, imitating Jimmi behind the wheel, I drove to a copy store, made my copies, then to the post office in Venice, running lights and screaming at the other drivers.

From a list of high-end men's magazines in *The Writer's Market* I bought stamps and mailed off seven copies of 'Compatibility'.

On the way back, I became more cautious. What if a publisher accepted the story, but I was arrested? I'd be in jail doing eighteen months for my second drunk driving, unable to get the acceptance letter at my P.O. box. A published short story writer rotting away at Wayside Honor Farm. Also, it had been over an hour, and I needed a drink badly.

Alone again at the motel, I drank more, finishing the quart on the night table, then part of another.

This was the onset of madness. For hours, there was only raging in my sober brain. I was waiting for something, I knew not what. Drowning in the fear of something not understand-able. It wasn't Jimmi. She was dead to me. Gone forever.

Finally, as a solution – a distraction – I remembered a porno arcade on Century Boulevard a mile and a half from the airport. Fifteen minutes away.

I dressed and was about to leave my motel room when, opening my door, I saw three pink phone-message slips left for me by the manager. All from Cynthia. Then I knew what was wrong: I had sinned against the memory of the woman I loved. I had caught this curse of sadness from Cynthia, this overpowering melancholy. This living death.

I had been to the porno place a few times before I got sober and started my vacuum cleaner job, giving away coupon books in Glendale.

I was always drunk when I went in. A dark parking lot in back and a small black and white sign above the door identified the building with one word: VIDEO.

Inside, a large, semi-lit room with porno magazines and empty for-rent movie boxes displayed on tall wire racks. Guys roaming around, cruising, staring at each other's crotch. On the far wall was a curtain and a doorway. Through the door was where the action took place. Little phone-booth sized cubicles with a chair and a TV screen in each one. Inside the booth, next to the screen, vending slots for coins and dollar bills. Not locking the door to the booth is the signal. Eventually, one of the guys cruising the hall comes along and finds the unlocked door. Wordlessly, they enter, get on their knees, and suck you off.

I stayed in my booth for half an hour, watching the porn, feeding dollars into the slot, then got a long, slow blow job.

On my way back to the Prince Carlos, I pulled off the freeway and bought another bottle. I was less tense. Now, I hoped, I could stay drunk and drown my life.

Leaving the liquor store, across the parking lot, I saw a pay phone. I thought of Jimmi and felt the sensation of glass shattering within my chest. Unable to stop myself, a fistful of quarters in my hand, I began dialing her number again and again, hanging up each time after her sister's answering machine would click on.

At The Prince Carlos, sitting on my bed, exhausted – undrunk again – I decided to try to write. Not another moronic letter to Jimmi, something else. I began with the pen and a legal pad but soon discovered that my hands wouldn't cooperate from the booze. Keeping the scrawl between the lines was impossible. I switched to Jonathan Dante's portable typewriter, propping it between my legs for better results. My fingers began hitting the keys one at a time.

To my surprise, words started spilling out. An old, sad memory. Not about Jimmi or anything to do with Jimmi. A recollection about me and a girl in a store – a donut shop.

I was living on Fifty-first Street in New York at a rooming house off Eighth Avenue. Her name was Yee. She worked afternoons and nights at her parents' shop near the Columbus Circle Subway Station. A part-time computer student. Yee's mother and father were old-country Chinese. They handled the early morning and day shift. I became a patron the day I started my new six p.m. job, a phone-sales hustle, setting appointments and demoing funeral services at Gowan, Fitzsimmons & Sons Mortuary *on Columbus Avenue. I would stop in, dressed in the required uniform, a black suit and tie and black shoes. I would stop in, buy my bagel and coffee to go, then catch the 'D' Train uptown to Eighty-sixth*

Street. Sometimes I'd have a buzz going, sometimes not, but I always bought the same thing. And Yee always smiled. It went on that way for a few nights. Being new in the bereavement business, unsure of myself, I practiced on Yee. She enjoyed my formal, exaggerated good manners, bowing when I bowed, playing along. Shaking my hand. Her smile had a gentleness from a galaxy a billion miles away from Taipei or the 'IND' Subway Station. When she would bend forward, reaching into the glass case to get my bagel, her hard, small-nippled breasts would show themselves in the gap in her uniform blouse ... One night when I came in, the baked-goods case was empty. Until then, our conversations had never exceeded a minute or two. I poured myself serve-yourself coffee and waited for Yee to finish taking care of another customer. When she was done, seeing me, she walked down the counter to where I was standing. 'Hello,' she said, bowing, smiling, mimicking my mortician-trainee stiffness. 'Hey,' I said playfully, 'you're out of bagels.' She stepped closer, pressing herself against the counter. From within the pocket of her white jacket, she removed a clump of carefully-folded waxed paper, then slid it toward me across the glass. 'I save for you,' she whispered. 'I know you come.' ... A little startled by the kindness, I unfolded the offering. 'Thanks,' I said, seeing the bagel. It felt like a birthday gift. Yee beamed, 'See! You special customer. My special customer.' ... I didn't say anything, worried for fear my incautious tongue might sabotage the moment by dispensing some smart-assed, gratuitous idiocy. Instead, instinctively, formally, I extended my mortician's hand. Yee shook it. It was then that our eyes met, really connected. I knew. Yee knew too. Zammo! ... The next few nights our greetings went by with us grinning and shaking hands some more. On Sunday night, the end of

Yee's week, I waited at the register after paying. 'I want to take you out on a date,' I half-blurted; 'to a movie.' Yee glowed; her magic, shy smile. 'I never go to movie,' she said. 'Okay . . .' I replied. 'That's okay. But do you want to go?' I'd made her uncomfortable and she began re-stacking coffee lids. Then the smile was back. 'Okay, yes,' she said, then nodded, 'I go. Thank you very much for ask me, Bruno. I go.' . . . The following afternoon I called in sick to my supervisor, Lawrence, at the funeral parlor, got a warning because I had already missed two days on account of illness, then walked uptown on Eighth Avenue in the honking bumper-to-bumper rush hour traffic. I was mostly sober except for a few beers, and my pants were pressed and fresh from the cleaners, and my shirt was new. Not a starched, bereavement-demo work shirt, but a twenty-five dollar blue cotton deal with jazzy buttons. Turning the corner at Fifty-eighth Street, I walked into the shop . . . Yee's father was behind the counter. Not Yee. I assumed she was in the back room. Pop recognized me and looked away. We'd seen each other a few times. 'Hello, Mister Chin,' I said, holding out my hand, trying for cheerfulness. 'Nice to see you.' He ignored me, keeping his attention on the register. 'You want bagel?' . . . 'Is Yee here? I asked. . . . Pops was stone. 'Yee off today. Not here.' . . . Unsure of what to do, attempting to conceal my disappointment, I nodded okay . . . But after he rang me up, I tried again: 'Mister Chin,' I said, 'Yee told me she would be here. We're supposed to be going to the movies.' . . . Two black darts bored into my forehead. 'Yee off.' . . . 'I know. I'm here to pick her up.' . . . 'I say to you, Yee not here. I say Yee off.' . . . Paying for my order, I took the bag and walked out . . . For the next hour, covered by the shadows of the subway entrance across the street, I waited, sipping *my coffee, smoking cigarettes, watching the donut shop's door. Yee never appeared . . . The next day I was early at the shop, two hours before work. From my hideout across the street, I watched Mom and Pop behind the counter, as usual. Shift change time, five thirty, Mom went home and Pop stayed. No Yee. Now I was crazy . . . I had been drinking most of that day and realized too late I had forgotten to call in sick again. It didn't matter. I hated my fraudulent body-bag job; the manipulation and pretense. Lawrence, my supervisor, was a flatulent asshole. Always making some correction in my demeanor, giving me 'notes' on the way I 'conducted' myself with this customer or that. Fuck him and all the necrophiliac sour-faced fucking ghoul cocksuckers who spend their days and nights hoodwinking the bereaved, up-selling, claiming a coffin was mahogany when it was really plastic laminate . . . I crossed the street and entered the shop, determined to see Yee again. Unwilling to take NO for an answer . . . Standing at the counter, I faced old man Chin. I wanted to let him know things were different. I spoke bluntly, 'I'll have a dozen donuts,' I said. 'And coffee to go' . . . Chin eyed me. 'No bagel?' . . . 'No sir,' I shot back, determined to break the rhythm of our absurd, former communications. 'And . . . I want to speak to Yee. Is she here?' . . . 'You want me pick donut — or you pick?' . . . 'You pick,' I blurted . . . When Pop was done, he pushed the pink cardboard box toward me across the glass. 'Three seventy-five.' . . . I handed him a ten. 'Mr Chin, is Yee here? Yes or no?' . . . 'Daughter not work now.' . . . 'I can see that. Is she okay?' . . . No answer. 'Three dollar-seventy-five!' . . . Pop laid my change on the counter. I scooped it up. 'Okay,' I called out, not knowing what else to do, 'two dozen more.' . . . 'Two dozen? You want two dozen? What kind you want?' . . . It felt good to be in control. 'It's of no consequence, Mister Chin. Mix 'em up. Two dozen. Sprinkles, glazed, chocolate caramel. And toss in a few buttermilk bars. And those three cupcakes on the end. The ones with the pink icing.' . . . After the new box was filled and wrapped with string, Pop punched the register. 'Two dozen! Seven dollar!' . . . I slapped down a new twenty. 'What about Yee, Mister Chin?' . . . No answer. The embalmed glance of the forever silent . . . I would not be deterred. Glancing down at the donut case I estimated that it was three-fourth's empty. Most of what remained was on the top shelves. Specialty stuff: eclairs, oversized glazed bear claws, lemon puffs, fruit tarts of different colors, and a dozen or so wrapped canoli-looking cream-filled numbers. 'I'll take everything on those shelves,' I said, pointing across the glass . . . Pop didn't move. He folded his arms across his chest. 'Daughter go school. College. No come back.' He pushed my twenty back across the glass. There was a gentle smile on his face. Yee's smile. 'You go now.' . . . That was it. He was gone. Into the recesses of the back room, to the secret place where heat and flour and sugar combine to formulate perfect confection. I never saw Yee again.*

Sometime after midnight I got to my feet, dressed, and walked to the pay phones next to the manager's office. I couldn't stop myself. Jimmi answered before the first ring, about to dial out herself: '. . . Who's this? . . . Flaco, izat you?'

'Jimmi?'

'Bruno? . . . Jesus!'

'. . . How are you?'

'Wha' chu want, man? I thought you was somebody else.'

'I want to talk.'

'Sept I don't wanna talk wichu. Go piss on somebody else's life, man.'

'Are you okay?'

'Why?'

'Hey, I got fired too. Remember?'

'You crazy, an shit. Okay? You callin' me fifty-fuckin'-times-a day. You 'bout the craziest motherfucker in Venice. Wors iz, you act so high n' mighty n' shit – like you're some kina shopping-cart-fuckin' rock star.'

'I just wanted to check in. To talk.'

'I know whachu wan, man. Bah tha shit ain gonna happen.'

'Can we be friends?'

'I knew this girl in my detox, the last time – homie girl they all call 'Zippo' – when she smoke rock, for fun, if someone pissed her off, she used to squirt lighter fluid on their house, their trees n' cars n' shit, then light 'em up. She showed me how to burn stuff. You know, just stand there on the street and watch the shit go up. Crazy. You're like her, man. You don't give a fuck. You burn up everything around you. You don't give a fuck.'

'So – everything's okay?'

'My brother-in-law, another cabezón like you, wants me out. My rent's three weeks back. I'm broke. Unemployed. I can't get no dancing jobs. No man, everything's *not* okay.'

'What about McGee? What happened with him?'

'He got fired! Mister Kammegian fired him. You knew tha.'

'I mean about *you* and him? What happened with that?'

'Bruno. Jesus! I'm a lap-dancer, man. I suck dick for money. What do you think happened?'

'It was my fault. I pushed myself on you. You couldn't escape.'

'I need money, man. I'm all fucked up. You got money?'

It was in her voice. I could hear it. I had to ask. 'Are you back on rock, Jimmi?'

'. . . I gotta go.'

'How much do you need?'

'You got twenty bucks?'

'Can we get together and talk?'

'Why?'

'I just said why. To talk.'

A thud and silence. She'd dropped the phone or set it down. In the background, I began to hear other objects colliding and falling. A drawer slid open – slammed closed. Finally, she was back. 'Okay . . . Bruno?'

'I'm here.'

'. . . You know where I live, right? My sister, Sema's house? You dropped me off before.'

'I remember. I know the address.'

'Listen . . . park your car in the spot behind my bug. Knock on the side door. Knock twice. Bring me twenty bucks.'

'No problem. The twenty is no problem.'

'How soon?'

'I'm leaving now.'

The ride to Los Feliz from my motel was fast at night with no traffic. Thirty-five minutes. Santa Monica Freeway. Hollywood Freeway. Then the 5. The booze was working again, so I drove carefully, observing the speed limit.

Jimmi's sister Sema's house was on Rowena. 3373. A beat up twenties vintage craftsman with heavy concrete pillars supporting the porch's roof. Once an upper-middle class neighborhood, the dark street with its crowded, sweating sycamores, concealed eighty years of L.A.'s decomposition. Turning the corner to her block, the smell and taste of sludge was in the air. By morning, over the palm trees slums in Boil Heights, the fireball summer sun would re-ignite the smog. A city of thirteen million being choked to death one day at a time.

As I pulled in behind Jimmi's rag-top bug, I misjudged the curb and the distance, bumping a sports car in her neighbor's driveway. It wasn't a bad dent – not much of anything – but I didn't want any trouble, so I backed out and reparked on the street.

After climbing the front steps, I walked around to Jimmi's side door entrance. I was about to knock, when my dead brother Rick's voice began yelling inside my skull: '*Yo, fucko! Are you crazy? This bitch is a crack addict – a goddamn train wreck . . . Go home! You just smacked a fucking car. Get outa here, man! Run. Go back to your motel room – lock yourself in!*'

I knocked, then pushed at the door. It popped open.

Inside, the room's illumination came from a flickering TV screen. Jimmi was on her bed, sitting up, wearing a stretch top and shorts, her straight black hair piled and tied on her head.

Seeing her was always a shock. Her beauty. The dark, smooth skin, the deep blue blazing eyes. She was barefoot, smiling up at me, but not smiling. Long brown legs full-length against the bed's light-colored quilt. 'Hi, baby,' she cooed above the sound of a cable TV movie.

'Hi,' I said.

She was whispering, as if we weren't alone. 'Close the door, baby.'

Stepping back, I swung it closed. The air inside was worse than the Los Feliz smog: stale, like a box of damp sweaters in the attic.

I sat down on the bed beside her, competing for space with a dozen Barbies. '*Bob, have you got a pen handy,*' she giggled, clutching one of the beat-up dolls. 'You missed me, right?'

An impulse made me reach out for her arm. As I did, she stiffened. Close up, in the weird TV light, her face was strained, ashy. She found the remote, flicked the sound off, then met my glance: 'You want to fuck me, right?'

It made me feel like a bill collector. 'I missed you,' I said.

She passed me a stupid Barbie, smiling, still whispering. 'I'm, like, your addiction, right?'

I tossed it back on the bed. My mouth sped past my brain. '*My* addiction hasn't turned me into a half-dead, twenty-dollar trick.'

' "*Admit that you are powerless over Jimmi. That your life has become unmanageable.*" '

I got off the bed. 'I can be in Van Nuys in fifteen minutes. I'll get my cock sucked by a sixteen-year-old crack whore for ten bucks. For twenty-five bucks and two chunks of rock, I can fuck one up the ass. A pretty one.'

'Hey baby, be nice.'

I tried to kiss her, but she pushed me back. 'You're drunk, aren't you? I never seen you drunk.'

'I'm not McGee. I'm not a trick.'

'Okay. Shhhh. I want you to meet somebody.'

'Now?'

She covered my mouth with her hand. 'Quiet . . .' . . . 'Honey,' she whisper-called into the darkness, 'vente, mi corazón. I hear you. I know you're awake.'

Seconds later, a child appeared in pajamas, padding barefoot, noiselessly across the slatted wood floor. A boy. Small. Four or five years old, wiping the sleep from his face. He was easily as beautiful as his mother.

'Timothy, this is Bruno. Say hi.'

The kid smiled, hesitant. He was lighter complected, lighter haired, but with the same blue eyes as his mother. When I held out my hand, he shook it firmly. 'Hi, Bruno,' he said in full voice. Then, looking me up and down; 'What section of Los Angeles are you from?'

'Right now,' I said, searching for words, 'Culver City. A motel on Sepulveda Boulevard.'

'I know where Culver City is,' he said, thinking it over. 'I've been there. Do you know the history of Sepulveda Boulevard? The Mexican derivation? I bet I do.'

The boy had me off balance. 'I think I know,' I said.

Timothy didn't wait for me to go on. '"Sepulveda" was the name of the Mexican family that settled there.'

'Oh, that's good to know,' I said.

'Do you know what Los Feliz means? Me and mom live in Los Feliz.'

I had the answer. 'Feliz means "happy".'

'That's remarkably interesting, Bruno. But incorrect. To be exact it means "the happy".'

'Timothy, Bruno and I want to talk. It's late, mijo. Please don't ask a billion goddamn questions and give Mommy a headache.'

'What kind of a name is Bruno, Bruno? My father is Irish. "Timothy" is an Irish name. Are you familiar with the war in Bosnia? Mrs Bennyoff is Jewish. You're not Mexican, are you?'

I was dizzy now. 'Bruno is an Italian name,' I said.

'Fascinating. Extremely fascinating. Do you own a PC with DVD? We're on the Internet. Aunt Sema is. Aunt Sema is a teacher too, like Mrs Bennyoff. I've been reading since I was two years old. Aunt Sema taught me. I have two cousins that live with us. Both female, unfortunately. What's your preference in children, boys or girls?'

'Boys. I think boys are more fun.'

'Do you know where Guatemala is? I'm bilingual. How many languages do you speak?'

'Okay, that's it!' his mom snapped. 'I want you to take your blanket and go to sleep on the couch in the living room. And do not read your books or play with your Game Boy 'n shit. And no turning on the TV. Understand?'

'Okay, Mom . . . How tall are you, Bruno? My Uncle Caesar is five-foot-seven.'

'You're pissing Mommy off, mijo. Get going.'

He disappeared across the room. The angel-faced chatterbox with the nonstop brain. Even in the darkness, twenty feet away, I could feel him thinking, ticking, forming new, more frightening questions.

At the door he turned back, toys and books and blanket in hand, overcome by the urgency to communicate and gather more data. 'Excuse me, Mom, can I ask another question?'

'Dios Jesús! What?'

'Bruno, Uncle Caesar has a Jeep pickup. A V8. Four-wheel drive. Uncle Caesar is a painting contractor. What type of vehicle do you own? What do you do for a job?'

'I'm currently unemployed.'

'That's two questions, Timothy.'

'I have a Chrysler,' I said. 'A two-wheel drive. A Chrysler is a car, not a truck.'

'That's fascinating, of course. But I know the difference between a truck and a car. You have a white "NY" on the top of your baseball hat. What does "NY" mean?'

'It means New York,' I said. 'For the New York Yankees.'

'Last year in school we took a trip to the La Brea Tar Pits. I have a hat from then. Want do you think my hat says?'

'No idea.'

'J. H. Hull School. It's in the closet. Should I get it?'

'That's it, Timothy,' his mother barked. 'I warned you.'

'Not right now,' I said. 'Okay?'

'You're a New York Yankees baseball fan. Right, Bruno?'

'To the death.'

Jimmi threw a leg over the side of the bed in a threat to jump up.

'Good night, Mommy. I hope you sleep good tonight. I love you. Good night, Bruno.'

The door clicked closed, and the kid was gone.

In two easy moves, her shorts and top were off and she lay naked, amazing. Looking up at me. 'I lied to you, baby,' she whispered. 'I don't need twenty bucks. I need a hundred.'

Reaching for my crotch with one hand, she put her other hand between her legs and began rubbing . . . 'Pinch my tits, Bruno. I like it when it hurts.'

I got up off the bed.

'I'm gonna make you feel good, baby. C'mon, take your pants down. I know what you like. 'Mimber, before, when I sucked your dick? You loved it, din'chu? Promise me you'll come in my mouth, okay baby?'

Digging in my pocket, I came up with a hundred dollar bill. Flattening it out with my hands, I dropped it on the bed. Then I walked out.

Chapter Fourteen

NUMB, MY MIND nearly sober from seeing Jimmi, the sneering voice of my dead brother ranting behind my eyes, I needed escape. Relief. My Chrysler was heading back toward the Prince Carlos when I chose to change directions. To just go.

Years before in New York, as a cabbie, I had discovered driving as an escape. Late at night I'd learned to rescue myself from my depressions by rolling through the empty streets of Manhattan, alone, listening to the humming of the tires, hour after hour. Drifting. Safe. Solutions had come easily. Ideas. Poems.

I needed that again.

Taking the 5 Freeway into the 10, I headed east instead of toward the ocean, San Bernardino – stopping only for two quarts of Stoli at a two a.m. liquor store. Fifty miles later, at the base of the mountains, I caught the off ramp to the 15, up the hill toward Hesperia and Baker and Barstow, in the direction of Death Valley and Las Vegas, the openness of the wide Mojave Desert.

Hours later, deep into the murky hills, my brain felt comfortable. In front of me, a dotted line of headlights extended fifty miles onto the flat desert. A pure black night, stars popping above me like a billion sparks bursting at the same time.

When the rim of the sky began turning pink, I decided to pull off on a dirt road and watch the sun come up, then head back toward L.A.

A few hundred yards into the sand, with the main highway behind me, far enough out of sight, I rolled to a stop then put the car's windows down to let in the chilled desert air. There was half a bottle of vodka left on the seat. After taking a dozen long hits, I clicked the headlight switch off and killed the engine. I lit a cigarette and smoked it. No ghosts. Only stillness. *Not the roof of a house nor the eyes of a face.* Nothing. Immense, undisturbed, raw space. Perfect quiet.

I found paper and a pen in my glove compartment. An old order book from my vacuum job. I began a new letter on the back of one of the carbon pages.

'Jimmi,' it started, *'I stole from you tonight. A pair of your panties. I found them on the floor by your bed and stuffed them into my pocket when you weren't looking. I will never give them back. I will lick them and smell them and keep them in my pocket and never return them. When I die, they will be cremated in my coffin with me. I stole a lipstick from your desk at Orbit too. I'm keeping it. I love you, Jimmi. I can't help it or stop it. I have not ever felt this way about any woman before. When you breathe, I breathe. When you drink water or wash your hands, I am there with you. I came to you tonight knowing you do not understand or care at all for me. That is why I left you. You are beautiful and you are mine and what has happened between us has left a magic that has changed my life forever. I will love you, Jimmi. Your boy too. Your wonderful son. I love him too. We will be together. Bruno.'*

It was dawn. I was okay. I folded the letter up and stuffed it in my pocket with her underpants. Then I closed my eyes.

*   *   *

When I woke up, I was sheathed in sweat, convulsing and twitching. My first impulse was panic. Clearing my vision, I looked around. Great squiggly waves of incinerating heat were out every window, like huge, dancing, transparent snakes hovering above the weird landscape. My head was pounding, and a sour taste began swelling and choking my throat. I reached for my Stoli and took a hit. It didn't help. Something was wrong. It was a sickness. A terrible demon had taken possession of my guts and flesh.

Reaching for the key to start the Chrysler, pulling my body upright in the seat, I badly scorched my hands on the car's flame-temperature steering wheel. Wave after wave of the shakes hit. Convulsing, I could only wait for it to pass. Finally, when I could, I twisted the ignition key to the right. The car started.

Now I was shivering. Dizzy. I got the windows up, then clicked on the A/C. Air began coming out – a tepid, weak stream – like blowing at a volcano. But it was something.

When I flipped the car's chrome shifter down into 'D', the wheels lurched forward, then stopped. I was light-headed, beginning to pass out. In retaliation, I punched the gas pedal. It accomplished nothing. The tires spun, and I felt the car sink deeper in the sand.

A new wave of the shudders hit. Out of control, I felt myself shit my pants. My mind, disconnected – off somewhere watching – gave me one last oracular message: I was going to die. Right here. A sick, decomposing hog. This was hell.

When I came to, the car was cooler, my breathing easier. Five minutes might have passed or half an hour. Somewhere I heard thudding. Pounding. A person – a body – was at my driver's window. A cop or my final death vision. The thing was yelling through the inferno of heat, but there was no sound reaching me. A cowboy hat. Sunglasses. A tan uniform and a gold badge. I tried to talk back, but my mouth was too dry.

'Zurg,' the cop voice yelled. Now I could heard it. 'Zurg! Egofo, Zurg!' the noise insisted. 'Egofo ug wagga donnn . . . Groll jurr winnnerr down . . . Zurg!' I found the crank handle, then lowered the glass.

The cop removed his hat and shades so he could lean in. A huge head, drenched in sweat. Big, distorted eyes. Horse eyes. A crushed red pepper for a nose. 'Dug fallow dar muter stoff, zurg.'

I understood. My brain decoded the words. I reached the ignition to shut the car off. But the action was crazy. With the engine off there would be no more cool air. Why would I want that? I yelled back: 'No. No fucking way!'

'Zurg,' the cop demanded, 'Nift you doll chadd zur aggin stoff ug fallow gule der motor.'

'No' I yowled, now believing myself to truly be hallucinating, clumsily attempting to roll the glass up.

But the cop was past arguing. A brown, sweaty sleeve reached across me and turned my motor off. 'Sir, I'm the Highway Patrol. It's a hundred and twenty-two degrees out here. Do what I tell you.'

The tow truck driver, a strange desert inmate-looking fuck in rock-star mirror sunglasses and a turned-around Dodgers' cap, arrived and charged me ninety-one dollars and sixty-seven cents to spray something on my motor to cool it down then haul and pull my Chrysler by cable back to the main road. The guy talked to himself the whole time while he was hooking my car up. Me standing in the sun, watching, terrified – needing a drink – experiencing near-death.

After the crazy man took my money, he counted it three times slowly, stacking the bills on the scalding hood of his truck.

The CHP cop, Officer Essmann, was an okay guy. He gave me a quart of hot drinking water in plastic from the trunk of his black and white, then let me sit in the air conditioned passenger seat of his cop car until my body temperature lowered and I could stop trembling. As a taxpayer courtesy, he ignored the smell of the drying shit in my pants and let me know by not bringing the subject up, that he was choosing to avoid writing me a ticket for the empty vodka bottle on my front seat.

Essmann stayed in my rear view mirror for several miles down Route 15 until I pulled off into a rest area to clean up. I watched his cop car disappear into the wavy Mojave furnace.

After washing myself and soaking my head under the faucet in the bathroom, I lit a cigarette and checked my pants' pockets. Seventeen dollars. My Chrysler had only a quarter tank of gas to get me the two hundred miles back to L.A. Not nearly enough. But not having gas money was trivial. I needed a drink. My stomach was beginning to spasm and cramp from alcohol deficiency. Back at the sink I sucked in as much cold tap water as I could stand, filling my stomach. It helped. Then I got back in the Chrysler, hit the A/C button, and headed west. The first green highway sign I came to read San Bernardino – 189 Miles.

Approaching Barstow, my fuel gauge showed just above 'E'. I was beginning to get the fly-aways and more severe, jabbing, stomach cramps. My body began trembling and convulsing. I had to pull off.

At the bottom of the exit ramp, like a snake carcass in the dust, was an L-shaped shopping center, a pizza place, a gas station, and a Thrifty Drug Store. Beyond Thrifty's was a tractor dealer with a giant yellow and green two-story sign: Duke's Killer Tillers. On top of Duke's sign, a clock/thermometer reported the only meaningful news in the desert mall: 1:37 p.m., 119 degrees.

While I waited for a shaking spasm to subside, my brain assembled a frantic scheme. To make it work all I needed was a drinking cup.

Pulling up to a parking space in front of the pizza restaurant, I cut the engine and the air conditioning. Through the windows I could see two or three customers eating lunch on the enclosed patio. Opening the car door, I sucked in my breath, and stepped into the volcanic heat.

Just inside, at the first empty table, I found what I needed: a used, tall, waxed soft-drink cup with 'Mendoza's Pizzeria' stamped on the side. A red straw was sticking up through the plastic lid. Grabbing the cup, I walked out.

Across the parking lot, staying in the shade of the mall roof as I walked, I made it to Thrifty's. My gut spasming and cramping was now constant.

The big drug/department store was cool inside. Wonderful. Only one cashier and a handful of customers. I pushed my damp hair back and tucked in my shirt.

Empty pizza-drink cup in hand, impersonating a nonchalant shopper, I made my way to the liquor department. Next to a vodka display, after making sure no one was watching, I unscrewed the cap on a half-gallon jug of Smirnoff from the back row. Then, holding the fat bottle beneath eye level of the liquor rack, I tipped it down until my cup was filled. Sixteen ounces of clear joy juice. I spun the cap back on and returned the decanter to its empty slot. As I walked away, even before I had the straw to my mouth, even before my first hit,

I felt a wave of peace soothe my body, like a kiss from God.

For a long while I was content to roam the store's aisles, sucking back deep wallops through my straw as I went. Making the rounds of the different departments.

Always a fan of clever display advertising, I paused to admire a nifty five-foot-high fold-out of an actress's parted red lips in the makeup/perfume area. My brain envisioned the size of a cut-out erect cock for a compatible exhibit.

Greeting cards were next. Cleaning products. Microwave ovens and counter-top appliances.

A realization came. An intimate anthropological under-standing. Everything important in life could be found at Thrifty's. Everything. If one never left – a person could spend the rest of their life going from store to store in the vast California chain operation. All Thrifty outlets had a paperback best-seller section and were uniformly climate controlled.

Arriving at Soft Drinks, I realized that I was more than half way down on my cup. Working up a very good buzz.

It was time to make a health decision. Opening the glass stand-up cooler, I popped the top on a can in a six-pack of Schweppes Tonic Water, then splashed in a few ounces with my vodka. Sweet bubbles to help soothe my troubled digestive tract. I slid the can back in its place with the others and let the glass door hiss closed.

From behind me I heard someone clearing his throat.

Turning, I saw a person, a man. He was planted several feet away near a lightbulb display, observing me. A rat-faced little fuck in khaki work clothes, a carton of Benson & Hedges Menthol Lights tucked under his arm. The logo on his shirt pocket read: Duke's Killer Tillers.

He stepped closer. 'You going to buy that six-pack of soda, buster?' he inquired angrily.

'What?' I said, self-assured, my hand empty except for the Mendoza's Pizza drink cup. 'Are you speaking to me?'

'Don't lie. You just poured from that can of soda. Then you put it back. I seen you.'

'I believe you're mistaken.'

This further pissed him off. He scanned me up and down, then marched up to a foot from my chest. I was now able to make out the name sewn in smaller script above the *Duke's Killer Tillers* logo on his shirt. This was Duke himself. 'My ass!' he sneered. 'I been observing you. The manager of this store, Ray, is a friend of mine. A good man. A straight shooter. Around here, we look out for each other'

'How swell for you,' says I, a little goofy from my vodka. 'I'd wager that you and Ray have *observed* your share of serial killers and Shiite terrorist suspects prowling around the Arco Station or that pizza joint across the parking lot.'

Duke let his carton of cigarettes drop to the floor. He was ready for action. 'There's two ways we can do this, buster . . . The first way is the easy way. I'll ask you for the last time: are you going to purchase that six-pack of Schweppes?'

I took a long, slow hit from my straw. I was bigger than Duke, but I wasn't ready to have an episode of tactical stupidity come between me and a return visit to the liquor department. 'Okay Duke, you win,' I confessed. 'I made a mistake. I'll buy the goddamn soda . . . when I'm done shopping, okay?'

Duke pushed past me to open the cooler. He yanked the rest of the torn-open six-pack off the shelf. 'You're done shopping *now*, asshole. We're going to the checkout counter *now*.'

In for a penny, in for a pound.

Making our way up the aisle to the register, Duke stayed behind me emitting audible whiffs and rodent-type snorts. I deduced that the smell of the dried shit in my pants had come to his attention.

At the cashier, he dropped my stuff on the rotating counter, then made an announcement loud enough to be heard in Paper Products. 'This *customer* here would like to purchase a six-pack of Schweppes Tonic Soda.'

'Tonic water, Duke,' I corrected.

He grabbed me under the arm. 'Time to show the color of your cash, smart guy.'

The register girl wasn't sure what was up but scanned my item anyway. Two ninety-seven.

I paid.

Toting my plastic Thrifty's bag in his hand, Duke followed me through the automatic doors out into the blazing desert. 'Where you parked, buster?'

The sudden combination of heat with the vodka had me reeling. The best I could do was gesture across the asphalt. Duke handed me my bag of tonic water. 'Don't come back around here. Next time I'll call in the law. Do we understand each other?'

Although leaning against a pillar, I was able to salute Duke. Like one I'd seen in a Demi Moore movie about Navy skin divers. 'Say it loud,' I yelled, clicking my heels, 'I'm black. I'm proud.'

I could feel his eyes on me as I shuffled across to my Chrysler.

Starting the car, I backed out then rolled down to the Arco

Station at the end of the mall. While I was pumping the gas in my car – my last fourteen bucks – I glanced across a couple of times at the showroom window of Duke's Killer Tillers. There, through the glass, stood the midget proprietor, the rat-snouted protector of Barstow, glaring, observing me.

I decided to stall. First, I took my time wiping my windows with an available paper towel, then I went from car door to car door shaking out the filthy floor mats. That done, I emptied the ash tray. I even tried to check the engine oil for the first time since my mother had given me the car. It took a full minute to isolate the whereabouts of the dip stick. There, with the hood still up, I stole another peek at the tractor showroom window. Duke was involved with two customers wearing work clothes.

I didn't hesitate. Slamming the hood closed, I fired up the Chrysler, then whipped around out of sight behind the Arco to a parking space by the coin-op bathrooms.

Mendoza's Pizzeria drinking cup in hand, staying at an angle to Duke's window, walking in the shade, I hurried back to the entrance to Thrifty's.

Inside, I was re-embraced by the cool sanctity of the store. When the girl cashier spotted me, she appeared surprised. I waved. A public relations gesture. 'Forgot something,' I called out, grinning happily. She smiled back, and I headed for the liquor department.

It took only a few seconds to pour my vodka refill, then push the half-gallon jug back into its place on the shelf. On my way out, sucking at my straw, I yelled, 'Stay cool, y'all,' to the cashieress. She responded, a perky institutional reply; 'Thank you, sir. You have a good day, now.'

*   *   *

On my way back to L.A, Route 15 West was nearly empty. Safely numb again, an old Jimmy Reed tune came on FM, 'You Got Me Runnin''.

I hit the gas pedal. Fuck it. I hadn't been over 120 miles an hour in years. This was fun.

Chapter Fifteen

STANDING AT MY P.O. box, I read the return address on the envelope. Orbit Computer Products. A window envelope. I tore it open immediately and found a check inside. The shock of seeing the numbers was like the sudden sweetness of blended whiskey; $311.00. Four of my printer ribbon orders had been paid after deferred shipments. I was rich.

I dug in my pocket for coins. I wanted to call someone. Celebrate. Then I remembered. In my wallet I found Cynthia's number. Thinking of her fat tits, I dialed. With Cin I could drink and get drunk and pretend to forget about Jimmi and act like a writer. I'd bring a bottle and we'd talk about books and politics. And fuck. I had used her before, and now I would do it again.

I began dialing, but as I did her smell came back to me. The sadness. How it coated the walls and clung to her bookshelves like Egyptian dust. A needy, forlorn deaf creature living in a house on stilts. We were alike: two cripples with books in common. She'd be glad I called. We deserved each other. It didn't matter that she was old. I'd use anyone. People in line at the 7–11. Anyone.

The phone rang six times, then a machine answered. Cin was gone, the message said, back to Australia. A vacation. Her antiseptic voice reported her absence and brought back the melancholy in her face. Two months in Byron Bay. A friend named Kim, her message said, would be house-sitting in Laurel Canyon.

I tore the paper up that held the number, then flung the pieces into the air.

On my way back to the motel, after cashing my check and stopping at the market, I went by the pawn shop on Washington Boulevard. Jonathan Dante's typewriter had brought eleven bucks in hock. The guy remembered me. I paid him and got my typewriter back.

I was half-drunk again, so we engaged in affable consumer-type conversation. Trying to think of something to keep him going, I confided that my ship had come in. I was on a shopping spree. I yakked on like a fool, willing to say any type of nonsense to keep myself from returning to an empty motel room. To prove I was newly rich, I started spending. A thick harmonica gleamed in its velvet case. A collector's item, he said. A real investment. He was lying but I didn't care. I proclaimed my love of blues music and said it was time I learned to play an instrument. Forty-nine ninety-five. I shelled out more cash from my roll of bills.

We talked as I went from shelf to shelf examining his merchandise. I tried on rings and a gold bracelet and a withered leather bomber jacket. On the shelf with his stereo stuff was a CD/tape player with a box of CDs. A package deal. Another forty-five dollars for everything. Dinah Washington and Ray Charles. Early Sinatra. I took it all. An hour later he helped me haul the stuff out to my car.

Now there was banging.

Squinting, looking around, objects began appearing in strange color streams. One color was shit beige – the shade of my room's walls, the floor – but the other colors were new. Brown. Black. Crazy red too. Disney red. Everywhere. I closed my eyes.

More banging.

I was woozy from the wine I'd been drinking. Mad Dog 20–20. Weak too. Tired and terribly weak.

I looked again. The light beneath the blinds told me it was day again.

More loud knocking. Again and again and again. Finally, fully conscious, I yelled, 'Okay! Jesus! Fuck! Okay! . . . Whoizzit?'

'Diega . . . The day man-eye-yer.'

I swung the door open and went blind from the daylight. 'Okay – What's up?'

'Jou hab a kall . . . a womeng. Chee says emergencee. Chee says to tell you . . .' Then – a look of horror in her eyes – '*My gow!! wha hoppeng? . . .*'

Diega was holding her mouth, stepping back in shock.

My eyes followed her eyes down to my arm. Blood. Soaking my pants, my shirt.

Looking around, the floor was red too. The bed too. Red and dark brown. Everywhere. Red was dripping from my arm while I stood at the door. My blood.

51/50 is what the L.A. police call it. 'Attempted Suicide – Danger to Yourself and Others', is the charge. Diega, hysterical, began knocking on doors up and down the hall, dashing about – sure that I was about to die – which I was not. Finally, her fat ponytail Cochise-looking boyfriend, Miguel, back in the office muted the TV, got off his ass, and dialed 911.

There was half of an empty gallon of Mad Dog on the floor by my bed. My enemy; sweet wine. Knowing the police were arriving, I chugged what was left in the bottle, hoping that the stuff would stay down.

Blue men began coming into my room. Sirens. I swapped my bloody shirt for another one and held a bathroom towel against my arm. Several of my motel neighbors peeked in from the hallway. People I didn't know. Then the paramedics.

Diega was worse off than me. Crying. Yelling shit at fat Miguel in Spanish. One of the medics advised her to go home and eat a tranquilizer.

Twenty minutes later I sat on my bed watching cops shuffling around, picking stuff up, moving stuff, looking through my shit in the hope, I assumed, of finding dope and contraband. There is an immutable law that wherever cops congregate, more cops must join in. Thoroughness is a watchword in law enforcement.

A paramedic gauzed my arm and taped it, then gave me an injection. Then, just before they took me out, under *The Demon*, my Hubert Selby novel on the nightstand, I found a note. I had written it sometime in the night, in the blackout. The note was to Jimmi.

First I went to the County USC Emergency Room and was put on a gurney. The two policemen who followed the ambulance told me the charges again: 51/50. Danger to Myself and Others. I was made to sign a report.

My cuts were deep, not across, but up and down my wrist. But the bleeding had mostly clotted and stopped.

A guy near me, sitting on a chair in the ER waiting area, was named Marvell. A thug. A Crip gang member. When the nurse left the room and we were alone, we talked. He asked about my cuts. Marvell was on some kind of meds they had given him, but he was communicating okay, just slowly. He had arrived in the middle of the night. A drug OD. They had pumped his stomach, and now he was waiting for transfer. Crack and Dalmane. Marvell's next stop was to be the Forensic Unit at the Twin Towers County Jail – the whack ward where they collect all 51/50s. According to Marvell, who knew of such things, attempted suicides in L.A., like him and me, are sent to lock-down for a mandatory eleven-day hold and evaluation. A legal requirement.

I have been confined to jail nut wards before. Mostly in New York. These are terrible places: airless and small, one-room cells. At first you are tied to a bed. The bed is bolted to the floor. There is only one window, and it is in the door. Glass with a chickenwire center. A slot beneath the window is for food and meds. The stench of shit and puke and disinfectant is everywhere. The crazies in whack wards scream constantly, twenty-four, seven. Everyone is medicated to keep them acquiescent, but still the screaming goes on non-stop. I wanted no part of the whack ward at Twin Towers Jail.

I asked Marvell if he knew of any way to beat the mandatory eleven-day confinement deal. It took his face half a minute to take in the question, then answer. 'Got priors in L.A.?' he said. 'You got a jacket?'

'Nothing in California.'

'Okay . . . just one arm . . . might-could-be . . . an accident. What papers . . . you sign?'

'Nothing. Just the cop's police report.'

'Okay, don't say . . . admit . . . nothin'. By law . . . they got to let you out. Stitch you . . . let you out . . . the law . . . izza law, my man. Hole you till you sobers up – 'n cut chu loose.'

My doctor came in. Doctor Cortez. He examined my arm. Then a Filipino nurse with a mustache wheeled me to a stitch room, out the door past where the cops were waiting, to where I was examined and X-rayed and stitched. The pictures showed I was okay, no ligaments cut or tendon damage. They sewed me up and taped my arm. Three cuts – eighteen sutures.

When I returned to the ER waiting area, Marvell was gone.

Doctor Cortez had already filled out the 51/50 confinement form, and the police were waiting for me to sign it so they could leave. 'Attempted Suicide' was checked.

I refused the clipboard.

Marvell had been right; they couldn't hold me. Attempted suicide is two arms. One arm is an accident. Cortez made a face, then tapped on the window for the two cops to come and get me.

I surprised myself by the phone message I left for Eddy Kammegian. It was this: *'Mister Kammegian: Bruno Dante calling you from The Twin Towers jail. Downtown. On twenty-four hour hold. I don't know any reason why you would want to help me. But I can tell you I've had enough. I'm making a commitment to never drink again. I want my job back, Mister Kammegian. I'm asking for your help here. Please.'*

There were nineteen men in my jail pod. Many more came and went in the short time I was there. The Twin Towers jail has one centrally-located mirrored glass sheriff's position watching each floor of inmates. Sometimes hundreds of men. The place is huge. I found out that L.A. has the largest jail in the world.

My body was withdrawing from alcohol. Shaking violently, I spent most of the next ten hours puking into a seatless, stainless steel shitter. In the middle of the night, one of the 'brothers' got involved in a game of *'toss-my-salad'* with a bald, ex-school teacher from El Segundo, while two of his bunkmates kept watch. *'Salad-tossing'* is a jailhouse amusement where the 'volunteer' is made to lick food – popcorn or peanuts – out of another man's asshole, then suck his cock. The cum is the salad dressing.

The bald teacher from El Segundo was punched in the head many times until he had licked all the blood and salad dressing off the jail's concrete floor.

The next morning at dawn – five fifteen a.m. – the owner of Orbit Computer Products himself appeared. Not Doc Franklin or Frankie Freebase or one of the company's admin flunkies. I nearly crashed into Kammegian as I was walking, head down, coming through the one-way hissing double-door exit. The big man stood in the middle of the hallway like a cement post, his thick neck stuffed inside a two thousand dollar attorney-looking pinstriped suit.

At my jail release I signed for my clothes and was also given a bill for hospital services: stitches, blood tests and X-rays, and the examination. One thousand four hundred and seventy-one dollars.

On the freeway ride back to Kammegian's house in Santa Monica Canyon, my withdrawals were still extreme. Constant tremors and stomach cramps. Eddy K kept silent the whole way.

Upstairs in back of his house, above the garage, was a converted weightroom/studio apartment. Unlocking the door, Kammegian pushed it open with his foot. A big, open room, musty and chilled in the early-morning light. But anything was better than where I had been. There was an exercise machine, a futon bed, a bathroom and shower, a microwave oven, stained carpet, and a black dial phone with a metal lock to prevent his guests from making outgoing calls.

Kammegian tugged open a casement window, then sucked in a mouthful of clean air. 'Shake it out, Dante,' he ordered. 'Get some sleep.'

I nodded.

'Feeling any better?'

'Like death. Awful.'

'I'll bring you fresh sheets and towels and orange juice and honey and some canned food from downstairs. You'll be okay. Half a dozen men have sobered up right here on that couch.'

There was something different for me this time. Beyond the puke stink and my filthy clothes and the humiliation. I felt crushed. Old. I was sure I was done. I tried to tell Kammegian. To say the words. 'I'm okay,' I said, my body rattling badly, making my way to the couch, easing myself down. 'I'm ready. I mean it. I want you to understand – I really mean it.'

For the first time, as people, we connected. Big-necked Kammegian folded his arms across his chest. 'I believe you. When a man says he's *ready*, I'll do whatever I can.'

'Can I have my job back?'

'You tell me something. Tell me what you think the difference is between us – you and me?'

Out of answers, I shook my head. 'No idea.'

'Faith is the difference. Willingness and belief. Other than that, we're exactly alike.'

'Look, I'm ready. That's all I know.'

'An alcoholic has to be desperate in order to recover. Pain is the key. Your pain is the beginning of change. Faith follows the pain and desperation. If you really want to, one day at a time, you never have to take another drink. That's how it works.'

'I'm desperate. I know that.'

'Will you trust me? Will you do exactly as I say?'

'Sure,' I said. There was nothing left to lose. 'Okay.'

'Good. Sleep now. I'll send someone from the office to your motel to pick up your clothes. In a couple of days when you're better, you'll start riding to work with me. Call Liquor Store Dave. Tell Dave I'm your boss again – and your new AA sponsor. Questions?'

I didn't have any. 'Thank you,' I said.

From a desk drawer, Kammegian pulled a yellow legal pad, a pen, and The Big Book of Alcoholics Anonymous. 'Direction number one: read this, the first one hundred sixty-four pages. Then write about Step One, what you think being *powerless* over alcohol is, what an *unmanageable life* is.'

I hated the fucking AA Big Book. I'd read it three different times cover to cover, studied it in endless group sessions in half a dozen different recovery programs. The story of Bill Wilson's Jesus conversion from bourbon whiskey after sobering up in a nut ward seventy years ago. Trite. Arcane, hackneyed bunk. The manifesto of an unemployed, busted-out, egomaniac stockbroker. But shivering now, looking up at Eddy Kammegian, there were no '*no's*' left in my mouth. 'You'll have it tomorrow,' I said.

On the floor at the end of the bed was an ugly green plastic waste basket. The big man yanked the liner bag out, then kicked it toward me. 'Puke in that,' he said. 'And clean yourself up. You stink, Bruno. You stink like hell.'

For the next eighteen hours I wrapped myself in a ball, shook and slept. When I could, I read Eddy Kammegian's used copy of Alcoholics Anonymous and guzzled orange juice, ate slices of bread with mayonnaise, and took hot showers. Somewhere in all the madness my head became quiet. The voice of dead Rick Dante was gone. Silent.

Chapter Sixteen

THE APARTMENT WAS on Twenty-seventh Place in Venice. Number 12A. Up a flight of brick stairs. The corner of Speedway, a hundred feet from the beach. Two bedrooms. The view was my reason for signing the lease. Great wide windows looking out at an endless Pacific Ocean.

Thirty days after my return to work, the stitches were out and my wrist cuts were healed. On the phone I'd been selling like a man possessed, my one aim was to prove myself to Eddy Kammegian. To show him I was serious.

It was a Saturday, seven a.m. My boss and Doc Franklin and eight other receiving alkie employees teamed together to help me move in to my new place. Kammegian had dubbed these guys his Orbit relocation SWAT Team.

We converged at my new apartment building with a rented truck loaded with furniture. A king-size bed and frame came from Doc's garage, along with a desk for my typewriter. The leather couch, pots and pans and dishes, and two tall oak bookcases I'd bought myself from a second-hand store on Venice Boulevard. A table and chairs were donated by Eddy's secretary, Elaine. The only unused piece of furniture was the TV; a big thirty-five-inch job. I'd put five hundred down on it. The owner of Orbit Computer Products co-signed for the balance – another thousand dollars – to help me re-establish my credit.

With Eddy Kammegian barking orders, the whole move was done in under two hours.

There was no bullshit in my boss. His commitment to his employees and recovery was absolute. On our way back from returning the rental truck, Doc Franklin and I talked. It was then that I finally learned Eddy's story, the beginning of Orbit Computer Products. As it turned out, Eddy K's early circumstances had been similar to my own. Just worse. Kammegian grew up, adopted, in Ghost Town in Venice, a shithole of a neighborhood, even then. By fifteen he had quit school and was hanging with bikers, sucking back brown-bag Nightrain wine. At twenty-six he began a thirty-month sentence in the slam for dealing dope. After release, on parole and jobless, is when his life changed. One morning, after a two-hour bus ride from L.A., tattooed, long-haired, Kammegian answered a phone-sales job ad in *The L.A. Times*. A telemarketing bucket shop on Van Nuys Boulevard. Pens and pencils. No one, least of all Eddy himself, would have believed what happened. By quitting time that day, he had earned five hundred dollars in commissions. Shazam!!

When the move-in was done and the other guys were gone, me and my boss stood alone at my window above Venice Beach. This was my first apartment, by myself, in years. The phone and utilities in my name. The heat of the weekend day was already beginning to drive an inland tidal wave of cars, filled with a hundred thousand sweating bodies, toward the sea.

In a parking lot north of my building, the first beachies were arriving. Looking down, we saw a dozen teenage Asian kids, tapping a soccer ball back and forth, make their way across the sand. Two of the guys, gang members in head bands, were carrying forty-ounce beer bottles. Already half drunk. They were arguing and pushing. Their girlfriends, wearing thong bikinis, looked on.

Kammegian's face distorted as he took the scene in.

He turned to me. 'I want you to do something for me, Bruno,' he said. 'A favor. Sponsor direction.'

'Sure. What?'

'Do you know your way to the "Hollywood" sign, in the hills?'

'At the top of Beachwood Canyon,' I said. 'Off Franklin Avenue.'

'I want you to leave now. Get in your car and drive to the "Hollywood" sign.'

'Now?'

'There's a good view of Los Angeles from there. Above the freeway shootings and the porno shops on Sunset Boulevard. I want you to make a pilgrimage, Bruno. Will you do that?'

'Okay.'

'When you're on the road above the sign, stop your car and get out. Just stand there. Will you do what I ask?'

'Sure.'

'Fill your lungs and yell these words. Yell out, *I will never be a fucking loser, again!* Will you do that?'

This was pure Eddy Kammegian. Symbols of self-actualization and AA recovery. I stood scratching my face. 'No problem,' I said.

That afternoon, hours later, after I got back to my apartment from Hollywood, I plugged in my refrigerator, opened the door, and found a note along with ten fifty-dollar bills. The money was stuck in the fly leaf of a copy of *How to Master the Art of Selling*, by Tom Hopkins. The note read: '*Bruno; your move-in bonus. I'll see you at the top! . . . Best wishes. Your Pal, Eddy K.*'

It was five months before my fortieth birthday. No one, not my own father, or a wife, or an ex-boss or a teacher or a friend or anyone else in my life, had ever extended himself to me the way Eddy Kammegian had. I made a commitment to myself – consciously made my mind up – I would stay sober and give Orbit everything I had.

Chapter Seventeen

THE COMPANY WAS in the last six weeks of its annual summer contest, 'Paris for Predators'. Orbit had plaques and prizes for everything, but this year's two-month Paris deal was the biggest contest ever, the monster. Kammegian had a firehouse bell mounted on the sales floor and made each of his salesmen clang the thing when we wrote a fresh order. Team banners hung from the rafters. Loud, piped-in marching music came through the sales room speakers before work and at breaks. There was even a dart board with money pinned behind the balloons. You got one dart to throw if you sold two dozen or more of any product.

First prize in the contest was a round trip for two: ten days in the shadow of the Eiffel Tower. All expenses paid. Second prize was two weeks in Puerta Villarta, and third prize was a sixty-inch TV/DVD home entertainment center.

Orbit's top people were pushing hard to finish in the bucks. Eddy Kammegian loved the casino atmosphere. Tempers flared. Ego was king. Out of the seventy-five telemarketers in the running, the two men to beat were Frankie Freebase and Doc Franklin. Frankie was ahead with twenty-eight grand in confirmed, shipped orders. Doc was second. Judy Dunn, a pretty, ex-IBM printer division rep, was a distant third, tied with four or five other salesmen.

Doc had won the contest three years in a row but this year the worm had turned.

As phone guys, Frankie and Doc were opposites. Freebase was old school, like me – a relentless banger. He slurped coffee seven hours a day at his desk with the telephone glued to his ear. A bad-tempered asshole on most any occasion, contests made Frankie worse. He'd built a massive account base of one thousand active customers.

Doc was his opposite: loose and funny, never letting himself work more than a couple of hours at a stretch without a break. In conversations in the coffee room, telling his Internet jokes, Franklin affected the voice of an FM radio jazz DJ and referred to himself as 'The Doctor of Love'. Franklin was cool. Everyone liked Doc. But his real talent was a lethal ability at landing the big fish: huge orders. Having once been a data processing manager himself, he knew many of the top DP people in the industry and his account files included Orbit's five biggest customers.

From his beginning at the company, Doc had been top gun, just beneath Kammegian himself in personal sales. Until now. And his bread and butter client for the last four years was the giant: American Farmers Insurance, with fifty-three branch offices across the country. Franklin had the DP Manager, Milton Butler, at AFI's headquarters in Denver, in his pocket, 'tagged and bagged.' Over time Doc had manipulated steadily-increasing orders from Butler and worked American Farmers up to paying absurd prices for their supplies. Every August Franklin made sure that AFI's huge summer order corresponded exactly with the deadline of our company's contest. Nasty Frankie Freebase had been edged out twice.

But things had gone sour for Doc. For the first time in a decade, AFI's annual earnings slipped. Overnight, a directive came down mandating Milt Butler to cut costs. He was ordered to drastically limit his supply orders.

Naturally, shit rolls downhill. Butler's phone call hit 'The Doctor Of Love' like a sucker punch after the bell, and he over-reacted to the setback. Too slick for his own good and determined to salvage as much of his yearly commission as possible, Franklin shot an angle and 'created' a bogus sale, introducing a new product to AFI: a second-rate generic cheapo toner cartridge our company had been buying for years from Korea. The product cost us half as much from the Asian factory, but it was junk. Doc knew this, but selling it to Butler allowed him to cut our price to American Farmers on the cartridge by thirty percent. The made-up sale gave Milt Butler a reason to go to his Purchasing Department with a hefty supply requisition.

Then, everything backfired. An eight-dollar-an-hour bean counter in AFI's Vendor Control Department spotted the weight disparity between the contents of the two toner cartridges and Butler's requisition got red-flagged. The DP Manager had no choice but to follow AFI's New Product protocol and do a test study. His department was instructed to buy samples only from us and conduct a six-month comparison test. Snickering Frankie Freebase looked like a shoe-in to win the 'Paris for Predators' contest.

The owner of Orbit Computer Products took the loss in revenue from American Farmers as a challenge. Kammegian thrived on overcoming shit. Any adversity. His personality was equal parts Billy Graham, Tony Robbins, and George Patton. 'The Big Guy' began spending every day on the sales floor setting an example, slamming customers, opening new accounts himself, leading his troops. Within two weeks, between Kammegian's personal sales contribution and the hysteria of the 'Paris for Predators' contest, our company was back to having its biggest three months ever.

*   *   *

My recovery in AA and my success had become a priority to Eddy Kammegian. We attended three AA meetings a week together. On Tuesdays and Thursdays, at the end of the day, I was called in to review my sales and to receive a monograph on personal growth. I had homework too: books to read and tape programs. *The Greatest Salesman in the World*, *The Psychology of Success*. *Think and Grow Rich*. My 'In' basket was thick with magazine and newspaper clippings on self-motivation.

And, as a salesman, I was taking no prisoners. I had won the New Accounts bonus three Fridays in a row, and my average weekly commission was twenty-one hundred dollars. One Tuesday morning, on a fluke, from a referral to the data processing manager of First Gulf Savings in Shreveport, I sold four hundred and thirty-two re-stuffed Lexmark printer cartridges. The guy had an emergency and was out of supplies. A ten thousand eight hundred dollar commission. One call. The largest order on a new account pitch in the history of Orbit Computer Products.

The news rendered Eddy Kammegian delirious. He used the sale to further boost morale and paid my commission in cash the next day at our morning meeting. Ten thousand loose silver dollars wheeled in a wagon. Noise-makers and confetti were passed out, and I was presented with a plaque and a special momento from my boss's collection: his own personally-signed photograph of Dwight Eisenhower.

My phone rang. It was after midnight early Friday morning. When I answered, there was no voice on the other end, only breathing. I knew it was her. Like a ghost – a child listening behind a keyhole. I could feel her heartbeat. 'Hello,' I said again.

Still nothing.

Over the last several weeks, I had left only one message on Jimmi's sister Sema's answering machine; it contained my office extension number at Orbit and my new home number. There had been no reply until now.

I could hear traffic noise in the background, a horn honking. 'Is that you?' I said.

Finally, a ripple of laughter: '*Bob, do these toner cartridges go out to your attention?* . . . Guess who, baby?'

'I don't need to guess.'

'Missed me, right?'

'How are you?'

. . . No answer. More cars going by.

'. . . How's the boy? How's Timmy?'

'Timothy! My son's name is Timothy.'

'Okay, Timothy. How's Timothy?'

'. . . You got your job back at Orbit with Adolph-fucking-Hitler-fucking-traffic-cop-Kammegian. Right? . . .'

'Are you okay?'

More laughter. Crazy. '*There's a sale made on every call, BRUUUUNNNOOO, you buy their tears, or they buy your toner . . .*'

'What's wrong?'

'. . . Sema said you said in your message that you have your own place now.'

'At the beach . . . Where are you?'

'Hollywood. Here on Franklin. You should see this shithole, man. Junkies 'n weirdos everywhere. A billion cucarachas and no fucking air-conditioning. You. You'd look straight down your fancy writer's nose . . . Hey, can I tell you something?'

'Sure.'

'Guess what, man?'

'What, Jimmi?'

'I missed two periods. I'm pregnant. Guess who the daddy is?'

'. . . It's mine?'

'Don't worry. They want two hundred and forty-seven dollars at the women's clinic to take care of it. My appointment is for Monday. In the morning.'

'You think I'm the father?'

'Hey man! I lap dance. I suck dick for money. I had sex with one person in the last three months.'

'Rick McGee.'

'Fuck you, Bruno . . .'

'You sound high.'

'I'm sick iz what I am. Weak all the time. First thing; I need to get out of here. And I need a ride to the clinic on Monday. You got money now, right?'

'Money's no problem.'

'Man Bruno, this fucking dump! Disneyland. Ya know? Every time I open my fucking door to go down to the bathroom or the pay phone, some zombie crackhead motherfucker is breathing on me – checkin' out my tits – talkin' shit. I gotta get outa here. Okay?'

'Where's your car? Your bug?'

'Sooo . . . you'll come?'

'I'll come.'

'Okay. Now! Come now! Right now.'

'Is Timothy with you?'

'He's okay. With Sema and her girls . . . but they don't want us there no more. Caesar, my brother-in-law, made me leave. Hey, guess what, they gave my kid tests, you know. Sema took him to UCLA.'

'Is he sick?'

'My son's I.Q. is one thirty-eight! They want to put him

in special advanced this-and-that. They're making him a G.A.T.E. kid. Gifted And Talented Education. Sema says I have to put him in special school. Computers n' math n' shit.'

'Good news.'

'Remember the way we did it in my car, Bruno? That's when it happened. Remember?'

'I remember, Jimmi. What's the address on Franklin?'

'It's the Hollywoodland Motel. The Holly-weird-land. By Wilcox. By the corner of Franklin. I feel like shit, man. How soon will you be here?'

My red-handed clock at the other side of the bed blinked the time. 2:05 a.m. 'Half an hour,' I said.

The laugh again – strange, off sync – as if owned by another body. 'You still love me, done chu? You still crazy like a rat for me? Yes or no?'

'You're high, Jimmi.'

'Honk your horn when you get here. You know, easy: beep-beep-beep. Two – three times. I'll hear it, and I'll come out. But keep your doors locked, and done talk to none of these donkey motherfuckers. Iz crazy over here, man. Half an hour, okay?'

'Okay.'

The next morning, still sleepless, I called in to work at five thirty-two a.m, trying to time it right so Eddy Kammegian would be away from his desk, on the Orbit sales floor, revving up his SWAT Team. I'd waited an hour for Jimmi outside the motel on Franklin Avenue. Now she was asleep across my living room on the couch, curled up under a blanket, a ratty Barbie under her chin. She had come with almost nothing. A purse, her dolls, and a plastic bag of clothes. Timothy was still at her sister's house.

Karen, the receptionist, took my phone call. I lied, telling her I had food poisoning, saying I would not be in. After a long, stupid silence, Karen said she would pass my message on to the boss.

At Lucky's Open-All-Night Supermarket on Lincoln Boulevard, I stocked up on groceries and aspirin and over-the-counter nausea medicine for Jimmi.

I got home before six thirty. The heat of the day was already seeping into the apartment. Jimmi had relocated herself to the bedroom. Coming through the door, seeing her naked on the bed, her black hair splashed across my pillow like careless silk, my breath stopped. In the daylight her beauty was flawless. Even the room seemed different, remade by her being there. Her perfume was everywhere.

Crossing to the bed, I looked down, watching the steady, quiet, up and down of her chest, studying each detail of her. Fingers and arms had just been created for the first time. Perfection. Her hands, their length and elegance. The line down her neck to her back and ass. A Degas painting. It made me shiver.

Then I understood something. I knew why it was that I loved this woman. She was like my dead father, at war against her own life and time. Ten thousand disappointments would kill her as they had killed him. Living head-on against herself would kill her.

Her legs were apart.

I wanted to taste her flawlessness, kneel down and worship that place, slide my tongue far inside that holy door.

I eased my weight across the mattress until my face was there and began to lick, gently and slowly, afraid she would stop me if I woke her. The sensation caused her to turn on her side then come to rest on her back.

I began again. Cautiously. Working my tongue inside the wetness of her, more deeply, until I felt her body accept me.

She awoke but didn't stop me. 'Okay, do it,' I heard her whisper. 'Do it, baby. Lick it. Suck it. Do it.'

Chapter Eighteen

KAMMEGIAN'S VOICE WAS roaring on my answer machine. A bullhorn. I turned the volume down so it wouldn't wake Jimmi. 'Bruno? Pick up the line . . . Bruno? . . . Commando Dante! Storm Trooper Dante! . . . Are you there? . . . It is vital that we connect! I want to hear from you on my private phone number, ASAP. Call me the second you retrieve this message.'

It had to be done. I had no choice.

Pulling the phone cord across the floor out of the bedroom, I closed the door behind me. From the couch I punched in the number: a cellphone Kammegian carried in a leather holder on his hip.

'Bruno!' he barked. 'What's up?' In the background I could hear the noise of his phone-pounding telemarketers.

'I'm sick, Eddy.'

'Let's review our deal! Your commitment is to be at your desk – your command post – five days a week. Correct or incorrect?'

'I puked all night . . . at first I thought it was food poisoning. I ate shrimp from the take-out Szechuan place on Eleventh Street.'

'What's your ETA back to the firing line?'

'I have the flu – something. A fever. The whole deal.'

'Are you sober?'

'C'mon, Eddy. Do I sound like I'm drunk?'

'It's Friday, the best day of the week, and this company is in the home stretch of a major contest. Your presence making cold calls is an indispensable component. You are MIA.'

'I'll be back Monday. Tuesday the latest.'

'I want a personal call, a progress report, morning and night. On this line. No phone messages. Understood?'

'Understood, Eddy.'

'Do I have your one hundred percent pledge that what you've told me in this conversation is the truth? You have been completely honest?'

'Jesus, I'm sick, Eddy. Okay?'

'I will expect to see you at five thirty a.m. on Monday. I want two calls a day until then. Understood?'

'Understood.'

The drive down Pacific Coast Highway through Manhattan Beach and Hermosa Beach was much as I remembered it. A little changed, a lot of new high-rise construction, but still beautiful. It was further north, as me and Jimmi passed through Playa del Rey, that I had received a shock. Only months before, on marshland where I had seen a boy throwing a stick for his dog, there was now no trace of anything natural. The power of money, poured concrete, and political juice had erased the open land. California's bulldozer ecology.

Driving south, after Long Beach, the Coast highway begins to look as it did fifty years ago, in pre-freeway L.A. The towns that Bogart and Duke Wayne saw as they drove from Hollywood to Newport Harbor. Seal Beach. Huntington Beach.

In those days, if you lived below El Segundo near the ocean you were unplugged from Los Angeles; a lightyear away from the oozing greed and hysteria of the movie and TV business. Most of these beach towns had one gas station, a pay phone, a bar, and one grocery store.

We took our time on the ride. The Chrysler was running good. Only a week before, Eddy Kammegian, forever promoting success symbols, had offered to co-sign a lease for me on a new red Firebird convertible. He'd nearly 'closed' me at the dealership until I realized what I was doing and backed out just before I had to sign the papers.

Jimmi sat next to me, a Pamela Anderson Baywatch Barbie between her legs, sucking Pepsi and punching cassette tapes into my radio's console. Bob Seger, Wilson Pickett, Tom Waits. She'd been clean off alcohol and rock since I picked her up. She was trying. Our only stops on the ride were at Burger King to use the bathroom and 7–11 stores for cigarettes and more Pepsi refills. She'd thrown out most of her clothes and dressed herself entirely in stuff from my closet; my sunglasses, one of my white, button-down work shirts, my underpants, my Yankees baseball cap, and my new sandals.

The back of the Villa Capri Motel in Laguna Beach is right on the sand. A swank, upscale bed and breakfast. Every room has floor-to-ceiling sliding windows and a rear deck facing the ocean. Pulling into the parking lot, our view of the water at sundown was unobstructed; a hundred feet away waves from a perfect green Pacific Ocean slapped the sand.

The room rent is cheap for what you get: two hundred and thirty-five dollars a night. Four hundred dollars for two nights. I paid the clerk in cash, and he gave me the key to Room 109. His name tag said 'Stu', a middle-aged, soft-spoken queen.

Completing the check-in forms, Jimmi had to remove her baseball cap and sunglasses. Stu recognized her. During the week he did freelance photography, and they had once done a bathing suit shoot together. She pretended to be glad to see him – smiling her perfect, cerulean smile.

Delighted by the coincidence, Stu yelled back through a

door behind the counter. His boyfriend came out. Luca. A well-muscled Latino, twenty-five and fresh from plastic surgery and cheekbone implants. Everybody kissed and hugged. Stu gave Jimmi a business card and delighted in telling her how beautiful she still was, to please call him for more modeling work.

On our way to the room with our stuff I watched her tear the card twice, then let the pieces fall on the gravel walkway.

We were getting along good. While she played with the TV remote I had my nighttime conversation with Eddy Kammegian, still bluffing at having the food poisoning. I'd caught my boss in the middle of an AA meeting and could feel him wanting to make our conversation short, concerned he might be bothering the people sitting near him. We were done in thirty seconds.

After I hung up I began unpacking, changing from my street pants into shorts and a clean shirt. Jimmi was on the bed looking at take-out menus, still dressed in my stuff.

After the call, when I looked over, she was watching me, laughing, waving my roll of bills from the nightstand.

'What's funny?' I asked, my attention now on the perfection of her brown legs.

'You, big shot.' The sapphire eyes. 'You and your success and your fucking money. I guess I finally got me a rich, white boy.'

'For as long as you want. So, you're glad we came?'

'If I was a thirty-five year old fat bitch with three kids and a supermarket boxboy job, how close would I be to a flash motel in fuckin' Laguna Beach?'

'You'd be in canned goods stacking spaghetti sauce.'

Playfully, lifting her shirt, she cupped her naked, brown tits. 'That's how I see it.'

Before I could walk to her, she was heading for the bathroom. 'Chriss man,' she snickered, kicking off my pair of underpants, 'just go out and get us some food. Pizza or something. And something for my stomach. I'm taking a shower. Come back in half an hour, and we'll fix your dick then.'

'I'm easy, right?'

'Way easy, baby. Guys are dogs. Little boys. Your cocks do all your thinking.'

I picked up my jacket and my money from the bed. Of course she was right. Only for me it was far worse. She knew the truth, but still I was afraid to say it. To me, nothing mattered except her. Nothing at all. Not my job, or AA, or Eddy Kammegian. Just her.

Leaving the motel, I drove around looking for a restaurant to buy a pizza, taking my time. I found an open drugstore that carried the kind of antacid pills she wanted.

In my pants' pocket was three thousand dollars in cash, so I walked the aisles buying other junk too – pissing my money away. Stupid stuff. Laguna Beach tee shirts, folding beach chairs, a new Barbie in a box – Hollywood Legends *Gone With The Wind* Barbie – three different sweat outfits for Jimmi (different colors), a bathing suit, hats, and a gag greeting card. On the cover of the card was an antique photograph of two circus elephants, each standing on one leg with their trunks hooked. The caption read, '*If we were together forever dot dot dot . . .*' Then you open the card and the two elephants are humping. The inside read; '*. . . I'd want more.*' At the register I borrowed the clerk's pen and signed the card, 'I love you. Bruno.'

On the walkway back to the room with the pizza and my first

load of packages, I began hearing music. Seventies disco. Barry White. It hung in the night air like a bad fart.

The sliding glass door was open to Room 109. Stepping inside, I saw that the source of the noise was a blaring CD player on the dresser. There were bottles of tequila and bowls of lime and ice on the night stand. Four tanned boys in shorts, shirtless and shoeless, drinks in their hands, were moving to the groaning, repeating, lyric; '. . . *oh baby. Baby, baby* . . .'

The odor of Mexican reefer filled the place.

Setting my pizza and the other stuff down, I looked around for Jimmi. She was outside on the deck, twenty feet away, a drink in one hand, still wearing my button-down business shirt open at her chest, dancing, matching Stu and face-implant Luca, step for step.

Crossing the room, I yanked the plug on the music. I tried not to let the anger in my voice show. 'Party's over,' I called out.

Ending the noise got her attention.

Half stoned, eyes like two mescal pin pricks, she maneuvered her way back inside, then took a long time leering at me. On stage. Gloria Estefan with a mean attitude. 'Hey, c'mon guy, plug the box back in!'

I controlled my mouth. 'Tell your friends to go home, Jimmi.'

Coming closer, grabbing my hand, she slid her drink into it. A big, sexy, TV commercial smile. 'Vente, baby. Lez dance. C'mon, Bruno.'

I pushed the glass back then pointed at the door. 'You know my deal. Quit screwing around.'

Spinning away, giggling, she slapped one of the guys on the butt crossing the room, then disco'd in silence to the dresser and re-plugged the boom box. 'Thaz right, I forgot!' she yelled, defiant over the music, making sure she still had her audience,

'You're mister AA again! Charter-memer-CHIP. One of Eddy Kammegian's robots. A champion closer! No drinking, right, mister big-deal-hot-chit-genius-telemarketer! No partying! No fun! *You buy their tears or they buy your toner.*'

The eyes of the others were on me. 'I may not be much, Jimmi, but I'm all that I think about. My paycheck paid for your fucking dance floor.'

Moving closer, rolling her hips to the rhythm of fat Barry White's absurd vocal, she wet two fingers and pushed them deeply inside her mouth, then wiped the spit across my lips and chin. 'Heeeeyyyy Bruno,' she hissed, 'I'm habin' fun, okay? If you don't like my party – leave – take a fuckin' pill – come back later.'

I held up the room key. '*My* money. *My* rules.'

Jimmi let my man's dress shirt drop from her shoulders to the floor. Naked now, defiant, she pushed her bare tits against me. The boys loved it. Cheering. 'How 'bout this, Bru-noooo,' she demanded, 'shove your money and your fucking motel room up your ass!'

I felt my rage and tried to back off.

It should have ended there with me walking away. But as I turned to leave, my mouth wasn't done. It spit the syllables, 'No problem, crack-whore,' I snarled, 'you win.' Then, from my pocket, my right hand peeled off two crisp hundred dollar bills, wadded them in a ball, and let them drop at her feet. 'While you're at it, cunt, buy *the boys* a few hits of rock. Just so they know who's paying your bills.'

I slammed the door behind me.

Chapter Nineteen

ALONE, IN MY Chrysler, in the dark parking lot, I felt the knife in my stomach, the desperate craving for a drink. Shame and hurt ripped my heart. My need to inflict pain and destroy, always trying for maximum damage. I had come here to strengthen whatever was between us, to help her stay sober, to convince her to live with me. What a fool I was! . . . *But,* my brain screamed, fuck her. Fuck that bitch. For her, I'd lied to my boss and risked my job. Fuck her. She was poison, and I was a fool. I hated her.

For an hour I rode up and down the coast highway, my mind racing. I was desperate for a drink, anything to calm the screaming. Eventually, at a 7–11, I bought two tall containers of hot coffee, half sugar, and guzzled them in the parking lot. It helped me slow down. Then, after a few cigarettes and driving some more, I convinced myself to go back.

At the motel, the instant I clicked the motor off, I felt panic. I was sure she was gone. What an asshole I was. I had shit on my only chance to make our relationship work.

I hurried down the walkway to Room 109.

The door was ajar, so I pushed it open.

She was there, alone, sprawled on the bed, naked. Seeing me come in she turned to looked up. A drunken, evil panther, frightening and beautiful. The new Barbie I'd bought was next to her on the pillow.

The place was a junk heap of half-eaten pizza crust, cigarette butts, and empty plastic tequila glasses. A two-foot-wide brown stain festooned the center of the carpet and there was an odd chemical smell in the air.

I sat at the foot of the bed. 'Are you okay?' I whispered.

She wouldn't look at me. Grabbing a plastic lighter she made a clumsy attempt at striking it. Over and over, refusing to engage me.

After a dozen more tries, when the thing still wouldn't work, she glared. 'Whaz your problem now, man?'

'You're pregnant. Has that occurred to you?'

The crazy, possessed laugh . . . 'Soooo?'

'Can we talk about this?'

Taunting me, tipping forward, she snatched the book of matches from my shirt pocket. I handed her my cigarettes too.

Leering, she shook her head. 'I've got a surprise for you, big shot. Want me to cho you my surprise?'

'Sure. Okay.'

She struck a match. 'Watch!'

It was only then that I saw the can of lighter fluid behind her tipped over next to the pillow.

The bed was an explosion of flame. Jimmi was on her feet, jumping up and down, squirting the flammable shit everywhere. Laughing and screaming simultaneously. 'Fuck you, Bruno! Fuck you! Watch! Here it is, jou cunt! Here's what jou get, motherfucker! Fuck you to death!'

It took me a couple of minutes to smother the fire with the pillows and the bedspread and to hold her arms so she couldn't hit me and strike more matches.

Chapter Twenty

THAT MONDAY MORNING at ten minutes to nine I sat, parked in my Chrysler, in the smog and heat, in front of the Women's Planned Parenthood Clinic on Sunset Boulevard, a hundred feet down the block from the dilapidated Hollywood Cinerama Dome, my air conditioner blasting on high. I was waiting for Jimmi, a book of Saroyan short stories pinned against the steering wheel, getting out every fifteen minutes to shove quarters into the blinking parking meter.

In rush hour, old Hollywood looked more unhappy than ever. A transient bus station of a town. Aging office buildings, fast-food plastic store fronts, the odor of gasoline smoke everywhere. Two doors away on a boarded-up store front, the caption on the bottom of a nudie poster beckoned: 'Photo Models Wanted – No Experience Necessary – We Pay Cash.' On the Sunset Boulevard of the new millennium, a two-hour abortion held the same importance as tossing away a used Burger King coffee cup.

Jimmi was inside getting the results of her final blood test. Her new Barbie was resting on the seat next to me. Already one arm was missing.

My passenger door popped open and she slid in, flipping the radio to a rap station. 'Okay Bruno,' she said, stabbing out her cigarette, her voice shaking, 'fuck it. It's time. They're ready. The front desk nurse wants the money.'

Pulling my bills from my pocket, I passed her three hundreds. She stuffed them into her purse. 'I hate this shit, mijo,' she whispered. 'I'm scared. I hate this a lot.'

'Do you want me to wait here or come in with you?'

'Come back about eleven. If there's no extra bleeding, I'll be out in two hours.'

'Here,' I said, counting out more hundreds, all the way to twenty, then fanning the rest of the bills across the dashboard in front of her, 'take these too.'

Her eyes were black blow darts. 'What's up?'

'It's yours,' I said. 'A present. Keep it. Buy Timothy something. Do whatever you want.'

'Quit, man.'

I was facing her. 'I want us to make a deal,' I said. 'I want the baby. I'll pay for everything. You bring Timothy and move into my apartment with me and we have the child. Forget the abortion.'

Her expression darkened. She fumbled in her purse until she located an envelope, then pulled it out. I recognized the colored paper. It was the card I had given her, the one with the photograph of the elephants on the front. She tossed it on the dashboard on top of the money. '*Us*, Bruno? What *us*?'

I could feel the blood in my face.

'Open it,' she demanded.

'I wrote it. I know what it says.'

She tore the tucked-in flap open and handed me the card. 'Read it.'

'Why?'

'It says "I love you!" You gave me a card that says "I love you."'

'I know.'

'But I don't love you. You're not my husband. You pay

for me and help me out. We're friends. I'm never going to love you.'

'Move in with me. Have the baby.'

A second later she was out of the car, slamming the door, on her way into the clinic.

An hour passed. I walked to Starbuck's, bought coffee, and got more quarters for the meter. When I returned, Jimmi was on the sidewalk standing beside my Chrysler.

After I unlocked the doors, she dropped in next to me. 'Yo, lez go,' she barked, lighting a cigarette.

'What happened?'

'Man, I hate them fat-clinic-dyke-bitches.'

'What happened?'

'One rule, man. Here it iz; I go anytime I wan. If I decide, I go. No questions. I pack my shit up and thaz it. Okay?'

'Stay sober with me. That's *my* only condition.'

Her hand was extended. Smiling. Two business people coming to an agreement. I shook.

'Drive the car, vato,' she giggled.

'Where? Home?'

'No. Back toward the beach. Anywhere outa fuckin' Hollywood. I tell jou when I wanna stop . . . Hey Bruno . . .'

'Yeah.'

'Even after wha happened, the fire an' all tha shit, you're still crazy in love with me, right?'

'What are we doing?'

'I'm goin' chopping, babee. I'm spendin' all jour fuckin' monee.'

Chapter Twenty-one

BY NOW IT was clear that Frankie Freebase was unstoppable. Orbit's summer Paris for Predators contest was about to enter its last week. His lead had ballooned to fifty-one thousand dollars in gross sales. Already swaggering, Freebase had pre-rewarded himself for the victory with a lease on a new Porsche Cabriolet. The gurgling yellow beast – tinted windows and racing scoop – sat in space number one of Eddy Kammegian's new, exclusive Top Gun Parking Lot. Doc Franklin's lowly black Caddy occupied slot number two. Franklin was a distant second and falling further behind.

The CEO of Orbit Computer Products loved keeping his staff pumped up. With seven days left, our big week-ending half-hour Friday morning sales meeting would now be devoted entirely to the Paris contest.

Precisely at five thirty a.m., Eddy Kammegian clanged his fire bell half a dozen times, signaling the staff to order. This done, he picked up his mic and faced his regiment of telemarketers.

Predictably, the Paris for Predators leaders were called up. First Freebase, then Doc Franklin, and finally, in third place, Judy Dunn. Frankie, as usual, used the opportunity to strut and crow. Kammegian shook his hand, and once again presented the number one guy with The Leader's Sword for last month: a five-foot-long, gold plated medieval replica fucker that hung all week in the front hall by the reception desk above the scroll of past winners. Eddy K, a piano of snowcapped teeth, draped his arm around Frankie's shoulder. His voice boomed. It was an honor for him to present the Sword of Excellence to the number one salesman at Orbit Computer Products!

Loud cheering from the staff.

After the bestowal, Kammegian retold (for the new trainees) Frank's Rags to Riches Story at Orbit. How the two had first met at an AA meeting in a half-way house. The boss lowered his voice for effect. Freebase, at the time, was twenty days sober with no previous sales experience. Eddy confided that it was at that first encounter he had detected the sleeping giant within the mean-spirited little prick. The next morning at Frank's job interview, he had made a commitment to his own success and surrendered to Orbit's sales training techniques. No more stinking thinking. Frank DeRosa was a *winner*. A true champion closer!

More cheering, stomping, and noise-makers filled the sales department.

Things were going according to plan.

Now, passing the microphone, Kammegian demanded that Frankie himself tell his co-workers *how he did it*.

Frank's part was the easy part. Everybody on the staff was Eddy K's straight man. He began, as usual, by thanking The Big Guy for the opportunity that had altered his life forever (more cheering), then he gave the expected recitation on how he'd busted his hump for years and set his sights high and followed The Master Closing Formula; *make every call a sales call, try early in the sale for a close, close on every resistance, and keep closing time after time.*

But then Frankie began ad-libbing and strutting; throwing in stuff about how these days the new people at Orbit were *pussies* with their computer-generated lead sheets, how they didn't make enough cold calls, or work enough hours.

To illustrate how extraordinary marvelous and successful he was, Freebase unhooked his four-karat diamond tie pin and waved it in the air. He followed this with a recital of his personal sales statistics: a reorder closing ratio over thirty-one percent, twenty Fortune 500 clients, the largest account base at Orbit. Spit was flying from his mouth as he ended with a rant about his personal holdings which now included two condos, a boat, and a shopping center in Mar Vista.

When The Big Guy took the mic back, I could tell he was pissed off but fighting against showing any annoyance. Next, Eddy called on Doc Franklin.

Franklin was a good sport. So was Judy Dunn. They had endured this guff since the little rat first took the lead weeks before. Somehow Doc had still managed to retain his 'Love Man' facade.

He was about to speak when Freebase, who suddenly wasn't yet done, snatched the mic back and began taunting the Number Two Man. Loudly, jeering, Frankie Freebase demanded that Doc tell the staff how it felt to be number two.

To everyone's surprise, Doc was ready. He bullied the smaller guy aside, snatched the mic back, and raised both hands in a 'V'-for-victory gesture. 'I didn't hear the fat lady sing!' he bellowed. 'Better be careful, Frank. She might be just starting to clear her throat!'

Wild cheering from the staff.

From his inside coat pocket, Doc pulled out a wide red beret and slipped it on. The goofy hat fell over his eyes and covered half his face.

The sales department clapped and hooted.

Doc grabbed Judy Dunn and began dancing a tango. 'Watch who gets on zee Air France 747 to Pah-ree,' he hissed. 'It won't be *you*, fucko! Me and my lucky lady have already booked our limo for a tour of the wine country!'

Even Eddy Kammegian had to laugh.

The following Tuesday at four o'clock, the minute I walked in and closed the door to his office, I knew something was wrong. Kammegian sat stiff in his chair, staring straight ahead. In his double-breasted suit and diamond cufflinks The Big Guy looked like a pissed off, rich soccer coach. I dropped my sales records on the desk.

'Have a seat, Bruno.'

'Another good day,' I said, sliding into my chair. 'Five sales.' I was fishing, uneasy, trying to catch his eyes for a sign of what might be coming. 'Five hundred and twenty dollars in commissions. No prisoners. Rock solid deals.'

'Very admirable. Congratulations.'

'Right.'

He pushed my folder to the side of his desk. 'This morning,' he scowled, 'I had a rather provocative telephone call.'

'Okay.'

'Clayton Timms from the Monday night men's stag meeting called to check in.'

'Okay, sure. I know Clayton.'

'During our conversation, he mentioned that he had telephoned your apartment over the weekend about the change in time for next Monday. You have the coffee commitment at his AA meeting, correct?'

Now I knew. We were on the same page. 'Okay Eddy, I see where this is going,' I said.

Big Kammegian was on his feet. Fifteen-hour days and the pressure of the closing weeks of the Paris contest had made him more on edge and military than usual. 'Jimmi Valiente answered your telephone. The same Miss Valiente that used to be employed here at Orbit Computer Products. A rather unpleasant revelation.'

'I wanted to tell you about Jimmi, Eddy.'

'A crack addict and a trouble maker. A psycho hooker. Question: Are you drinking again, Mister Dante? Are you using rock cocaine with your girlfriend?'

'I'm clean and sober. We both are. We've been living together for three weeks.'

'When Clayton recognized her voice, he hung up. He's had dealings with Jimmi before.'

'That must've taken real guts.'

'It's a small world, Mister Dante. According to Clayton, before he got off drugs, he used to trade Miss Valiente dope for sex. She was living in her car at the time. It turns out she gives a first rate blow job.'

'That's got nothing to do with me and her.'

The veins were bulging on Kammegian's neck. 'The two of you are miracles of mental health!'

'We're going to meetings together.'

'Two cripples. The walking wounded. Jimmi Valiente will trade your balls and your soul for a hit on the pipe, then leave you bleeding on the sidewalk. You've betrayed my trust, Mister Dante.'

'No I didn't, Eddy.'

'We had a deal, remember? An agreement. Your commitment was to follow my direction to the letter. This was your opportunity to turn your life around.'

'We had no deal about Jimmi. We never discussed Jimmi.'

'Bullshit, Mister Dante! More evasion. Blatant prevarication.'

I remembered that my boss was an orphan. Once a homeless child on the streets of Venice. 'Jimmi's pregnant, Eddy . . . She's having my kid.'

The Big Man flopped back in his chair and sighed heavily. 'Splendid, Dante. And when were you planning on disclosing that fucking gem of information?'

'What would you have done if you were me?'

'It's called changing seats on the *Titanic*. You're a sap. *The beaver trail leads to wine country*. The last time you got involved with Valiente you wound up drunk in the emergency room.'

'It's different now.'

'Insanity! Making the same mistake again and again, then expecting different results.'

I stood up. 'Am I fired? If I am, I want to know.'

'Get out of my office.'

Chapter Twenty-two

THERE WAS ONE day left in the summer contest. That Thursday at three o'clock, with the sales staff gathered, Kammegian was awarding our spiffs for the day. Judy Dunn had sold five dozen 1403 printer ribbons on a reorder and made a six hundred thirty dollar commission. She came in first. She was given four darts to throw at the big, packed balloon board.

For the first time in a week, Frankie Freebase had come in second for the daily bonus. He'd only earned four hundred dollars in commission. And I was in third place with a solid three sixty.

With the boss officiating, we all stood in line waiting for our turn with the darts. His goading and cheerleading made Judy nervous. She was annoyed after throwing three of her darts and not popping any balloons. As she was getting ready to toss the last one, Doc Franklin, in his red beret, bounded across the sales floor holding an order. His smile was ear to ear.

'Hold that dart!' he screamed.

Eddy Kammegian took the order from his hand and checked the total.

The Big Guy stepped back, looking stunned.

'Doc,' he barked, 'is this deal confirmed and for regular shipment?'

Franklin was vibrating with excitement, hopping up and down. 'Signed, sealed, and delivered, Big Guy! You know me! Good as gold! No air balls for the Doctor of Love! Ever!'

Kammegian, order in hand, crossed to his fire bell and began clanging it again and again. 'My friends, fellow commandos,' he yelled, 'I hold in my hand an order. A massive order! A seventy-nine-thousand-dollar megaton explosion for paper and toner products from American Farmers Insurance!'

'Is this for regular shipment?' inquired the boss.

'Two week delivery, Big Guy! One customer, one call! I just got off the phone. I am the Doctor! Number *One*! The Doctor of Love! Milton Butler is my bitch forever! My mooch for life!'

The sales department was hushed in disbelief.

As Eddy read each column of the order out loud, the staff returned to life and began applauding. The quantities and totals were staggering, unreal. Doc's final commission on the deal was $35,052, his largest order ever. The Paris for Predators contest was now over. Out of reach. Frankie Freebase stood by, a handful of plastic darts at his side, speechless.

Chapter Twenty-three

WAKING UP AT night with Timothy in bed between us was hard to get used to. Jimmi always slept naked and walked around the apartment without clothes. It was her way. During the day we sent him to YMCA camp. The kid had his own bedroom with a used Mac computer but he refused to sleep there. Most nights I'd be up and down anyway, smoking, moving from room to room in the dark like a ghost, my mind haunted, obsessed with some crazy shit or other that wouldn't go away. I would read or write for an hour, then try to sleep again, going back to bed only to wake up later with the kid hugging me, attached to my arm or my leg.

Timothy turned six years old on the Saturday after the last day of the Orbit contest. For his birthday I went to Small World Books and bought him numbers one and two of the Anamorphs series by K.A. Applegate, a well-written sci-fi collection for pre-teen kids. The lady clerk said the paperbacks were advanced for a six year old and assured me of their popularity.

That night at home, the three of us were together with streamers, Hawaiian Punch, and a birthday cake. Timothy began opening his presents. When he got to mine, after tearing the wrapping open, he made a face.

'Hey, what's wrong?' I said. 'You told me that you appreciate fiction.'

The boy looked toward his mother but wouldn't answer.

Jimmi saw the Anamorphs paperbacks and smiled. 'Tell Bruno, mijo,' she scolded.

'No. It's okay.'

'I said tell him Timothy, for chrissake.'

He got up and padded quickly to his room and a minute later returned with a box. He set the container at my feet and opened the lid. All seventeen Anamorphs were inside. He piled them on the floor in front of me. 'I like science fiction very much, Bruno, but I've read these. I can assure you they're very engaging, especially *The Underground* and *The Escape*. I've read *Goosebumps* too. Basically, I guess you know, they're written for children. I'm sure you would agree.'

'Okay, then what about *Tarzan*? Have you read that? And *Robinson Crusoe*?'

'My favorite novel is *Stranger in a Strange Land*. I'm currently reading *Jurassic Park* by Michael Crichton.'

I pointed to my gift. 'No problem,' I said, 'I've got the receipt. I'll take 'em back. I'll keep Michael Crichton in mind.'

Timothy began re-boxing his Anamorphs. 'Bruno . . . have I hurt your feelings?'

'I look a little stupid,' I said, laughing, 'but I'll live.'

Ten minutes later he was gone, back to play in his room, warming up to scare the shit out of mankind.

To keep herself busy, Jimmi took a day gig at a stand on the Venice boardwalk. She said she hated lap dancing and that she was through. Too slippery. Her new boss was a huge Latino peddler everybody called Mister Jewels. He assigned Jimmi to a booth close to the Sidewalk Cafe, selling yo-yos and kids' magic coloring pens that changed shades as you used them. Her commissions were good right away; sometimes a hundred and fifty dollars a day. After day camp Timothy would meet her and they would work the booth together. Jewels was smart, always insisting that Jimmi stand in front of the booth, pitching the tourist mooches and the beach crowd. Even pregnant and beginning to show, the people on the strand would see her in her halter top, her amazing good looks, and be drawn to stop by and spend.

Our sobriety is what seemed to bond us together. Sometimes I would come home and find notes taped to the refrigerator. Some were funny. *'BD,'* one started; *'I bought us steaks on sale three pounds and rice and beans and lots of other shit. A hundred and fifty bucks. You'll see. Look in the fridge. Timothy made me go back and get him turkey hot dogs. Three packs. My kid's nuts. After the dentist another hundred and sixty-five dollars for two cavities he tole me he's now a vegetarian. Who knows where he got that shit. I think it was in a magazine in the waiting room. He won't say why he won't eat meat only that it's eleemosynary. When I asked him what eleemosynary was he said I should look it up if I wanted to know. Leave me more money so I can get more rabbit food for the vegetarian. Bye bye sweetie pie. J.V.'*

On weekend nights we attended AA at a meeting room called the Marina Center. And, on Sunday mornings, before she went to work, the big open air Venice Beach AA meeting.

The sex was good too. Eventually, off crack, when I didn't demand or ask, Jimmi just started wanting to fuck. But we never kissed, and she always made sure to say we weren't in love.

It became regular. In bed at night, after the boy was asleep, we would tiptoe into his room to screw. Her on top always, the room dark, arms folded across her eyes or locked behind her head, slowly, grinding in a circle twenty minutes at a time, her body shiny from sweat, hair stuck to her face and neck like locks of black seaweed. I was lost. Nothing had ever felt this good.

But still she was restless. I could sense her need for separateness. There was distance, a visceral anger. For a day or two sometimes, for no reason, she would avoid talking or looking at me and snarl at the kid. Occasionally, needing a change, she would stay out at night with Mister Jewels, drinking coffee with the tattoo people and beach peddlers from the Venice strand. I didn't mind. Because mostly it was good. Us living together was good. I knew time would make it right.

Chapter Twenty-four

LAS VEGAS IS a big cum stain, an upholstered sewer. Even as a drunk I hated it. It gets bigger and uglier by the hour, a shiny, oozing, radioactive oil spill, contaminating the Nevada desert. Jimmi got the weekend off from her peddling job, and we took Timothy with us. The trip was her idea. A girl friend named Laylonee, a strip-bar dancer, had relocated from L.A. two years before and was getting married. Not yet twenty-eight, it was her fourth shot at the deal.

Our seven o'clock plane from LAX landed at McCaren Airport in less than an hour.

Laylonee was stumbling, whacked on downs, Nembutal or valium. She and Mickey-o, the fiancé, a muscle-bound dufus, met the three of us at the gate. Standing talking, it felt like the perfect Las Vegas greeting. Jimmi's friend looked ridiculous and beautiful with her huge water-balloon tits, stoned, teetering in high heels. A damaged Showgirl Barbie. Boyfriend Mickey-o's idea of saying 'hi' was a syncopated grunt.

Making our way from the terminal to the parking lot, we resembled a Martian acrobatic troop. I held the kid's hand as people would notice us then stop in their tracks. Mickey-o was the problem – two feet wider than any other human in the airport. Even Timothy couldn't restrain his staring. The guy was an ox, no more than five feet tall, a squashed, miniature Thor, who seemed to have hopped down from one of the concrete pedestals in front of Caesar's Palace. His three-color elastic jumpsuit looked like it was painted on over his weightlifter body. The only unexposed body part on Mickey-o was his dick.

The bridegroom and bride-to-be lived in the Executive Suites Condos, a three-bedroom furnished by-the-week apartment deal behind the Las Vegas strip. Mickey-o stowed our stuff in the back of Laylonee's Range Rover, got behind the wheel, then swung us out into the bumper to bumper traffic.

I could feel Jimmi's anger in the seat beside me. Her girlfriend, who had demanded she be at the wedding, was completely zoned, too high to carry on a conversation. The roles of the two were obvious; he was her stooge, caretaker, and gofer. It turned out that all the wedding preparations and bridesmaids and the chapel had been left up to Mickey-o.

When we got to the apartment, Laylonee disappeared into the bedroom with a bottle of Cold Duck, turned the TV on, and closed the door. Her bouncer shuffled out to run last-minute errands. I assumed it would be up to Jimmi and me and the kid to walk or depend on cabs.

Right away, as I was setting our stuff on the bed, Jimmi talked about leaving. The deal was bullshit. But I voted to stay on because of Timothy. The boy loved magic, and Doc Franklin from work had called ahead for me to a friend at the casino who got us tickets to see Sigfried and Roy's illusion show. Finally, reluctantly, she agreed. And while Timothy played Zelda 64 on the TV in the patio, we started unpacking.

Half an hour later the woman in my life stood in the bathroom doorway wrapped in a towel, radiant, amazingly sexy, drying herself. 'Man,' she snarled, still pissed off and unable to change her mood, 'thaz me. In tha fuckin' bedroom, buzzed out of my shit, watchin' "Law & Order" reruns;

getting married in twelve fuckin' hours to an orangutan steroid goon.'

'That's not you. You're with me.'

Her hands went to her stomach, rubbing it through the towel. 'Right. Stuck with another kid. Just for a change, the short end of the stick.'

'Your choice, Jimmi.'

'Thaz ka-ka, man! Bullshit! You got a skill, a trade. Long as they make phones and printers need ink, and Eddy hot-shit Kammegian keeps paying off with bags full of silver dollars, your ass is covered. What I got?'

'We've talked about this.'

'Laylonee makes a thousand dollars a night in the dark, rubbin' her pussy up and down on some trick's dirty Levis. I got zip, man.'

I found my wallet in my pants on a chair. 'Okay, I said,' throwing it on the bed, 'go buy a yourself a bag of valium; you'll have just what she has.'

'You kno wham sayin'. What happens if you're gone? I got nothin'. A chickenshit peddling job selling toys for Mister Jewels. Thaz my fucking career path.' Grabbing her stomach. 'Not even medical insurance for this kid.'

Up to now, I had been afraid to say what had been gnawing at my heart. 'Okay, let's get married.'

'C'mon, man. Get serious!'

'We're in Las Vegas; it takes two hours. All we need is a license and a chapel.'

What I saw next made me choke. Jimmi let her towel drop to the floor. 'You'd do that?'

'My job covers medical if we're married. It's no less absurd than a weightlifter and a lap dancer.'

She was smiling. Affected. 'Thaz crazy shit, Bruno. You know me. You know how I feel. I tole you.'

'I'll take my chances.'

She was in front of me rubbing her brown nipples, pinching them with her fingers. 'Thanks, baby. Thatz nice. Real nice. It means a lot.'

When I tried to touch her, she backed away. 'No,' she whispered, 'jus watch. Stand there and jus watch.'

She wet her fingers and began to masturbate, one foot on the bed, looking at me, holding my eyes with hers. Rubbing slowly at first, then faster and harder. 'Seeee baby,' she breathed, 'this is for you. I'm doin' it for you.'

I unzipped my pants. 'Can I do it too? With you?'

'Do it,' she hissed, working her hand around and around in a circle against her cunt. 'Do it with me . . . do it . . . do it.'

After she orgasmed, I still wasn't done. She pushed me down on the bed. While she looked on, I began stroking myself. She pressed my other hand to her tits, then wet her fingers deep in her pussy, brought them up, and pushed them into my mouth. Licking the hand, I continued pumping. She wet the fingers again and wiped them across my lips. 'Taste my pussy, baby. Taste it. You're my man. Taste it. Do you love my pussy?'

I came like a rocket.

As we were getting dressed, there was a knock at the door. Then banging. 'Timothy, mijo,' Jimmi called, 'just a minute. We'll be right out.'

It swung open. Laylonee stood before us in the doorway, fully made up, black heels, wearing a tight top and form-fitting spandex. She had now gone the other way, and she was wired, a one-eighty from where she had been an hour before, popping her fingers to the rock 'n roll in her head. 'Hey sugar,' she giggled at Jimmi, 'your honey baby girl's getting married tomorrow. It's time to par-tee.'

The intrusion pissed me off. I was about to shave, my shirt

still half on. 'Sorry,' I snapped, stepping toward her, 'we've got tickets to a show.'

Two blank bullets stared back through me.

Laylonee hurried past me to Jimmi and began pulling her by the arms. Giggling again. 'Sure, okay, okay, no big deal. Five minutes. Five seconds. C'mon pregnant lady, at least come'n look at my dress. Cost me three grand. C'mon, c'mon.'

Jimmi followed her, reluctantly, being tugged across the carpet.

Five minutes became half an hour. Finally, shaved and irritated by the delay, I went out to the living room. The kid was still busy on the patio battling his video game. 'Hey,' I called, 'we have to go pretty soon. Where's your mom?'

He didn't look up. 'They're gone, Bruno.'

'What?' I said, not getting it, then noticing Laylonee's open bedroom door.

'A few minutes ago. Mom required me to tell you. She said for us to go out by ourselves. She'll be back later.'

'Where did they go? Did she say?'

'You know my mother, Bruno. You know how she is.'

'Fucking cocksucker!'

Still not looking up from the game. 'Bruno . . .'

'What!'

'I'm a juvenile. That language is unacceptable in front of a child.'

'Okay. Sorry.'

She wasn't at the wedding the next day at noon, and Laylonee hadn't seen her since some time in the middle of the night. Mickey-o had arrived to pick them both up at a penthouse in the Belagio Hotel. Jimmi wouldn't leave. She was having fun and decided to stay on at the party.

At three o'clock that afternoon, I was alone in their apartment with Timothy when the phone rang. 'Hello.'

'Hi Bruno, babee.'

'Hi.'

'How was Sigfried and Roy? How's Timothy?'

I could hear the cocaine in her voice. 'Hey, fuck you, Jimmi!'

'. . . Yo, chill man. Whaz your fuckin' problem?'

'For one thing, you abandoned your kid.'

Silence. Spooky nothingness. Finally, I heard her light a cigarette. 'Okay, look, take Timothy back to L.A. with you. I'm flying in tonight. Maybe later. Okay?'

'Where are you?'

'I'm asking for a favor, Bruno. A simple fuckin' goddamn favor.'

'What's going on, Jimmi?'

No answer. Her end of the phone had clicked dead.

Chapter Twenty-five

IN L.A., ON the way back from the airport with Timothy, I stopped by my P.O. box at the Venice post office. There, amongst the crap and junk mail and bills, was a letter without a window. *Boudoir Magazine*'s red logo was on the upper corner. I held it against the light, but I couldn't bring myself to open the envelope.

Outside, in my Chrysler, I handed the letter to Timothy and explained what it was. 'Okay,' I said, 'you do it. You're a lucky kid. Open it for me.'

'That's a ludicrous superstition, Bruno.'

'Just open it, please.'

Timothy yanked the envelope apart. There were two pieces of paper inside. One appeared to be a blank questionnaire. It fell to his lap. He picked the form up, examined it, and passed it to me. 'What's that?' he asked.

'A good sign. Keep going.'

He unfolded the letter. 'Shall I read it out loud?'

'Good idea. That or stab me with a knife.'

'It says, "Dear Mister Dante. We would be pleased to publish your story *Compatibility* in our December issue of *Boudoir Magazine*. Enclosed is our tax form to be completed. Kindly fill it out and send it back. Upon receipt of the form, we will forward our check in the amount $1,750.00. Best wishes, Carla Gould, Senior Story Editor."'

'Thanks, Timothy,' I said. 'That's all it says?'

He passed me the letter. 'Congratulations, Bruno. You're a magazine writer.'

I held it in my hands and examined its texture. I could see and feel the bits of fiber. It was laser printed on good stock. An impressive document. I studied the logo again and the signature on the bottom. Carla Gould. Carla Gould. Neat, tight, blue circles. Carla Gould. Unpretentious. Trustworthy. Carla Gould.

The boy was watching my reaction. 'Hey Bruno, you're crying. I assume you're happy.'

I touched my eyes and felt the tears. 'Yeah Timothy, I am. I'm very happy.'

When we got home, there was one message on the answering machine, but it wasn't from Jimmi. Doc Franklin from work had called late Friday night, hoping I was still in town, sounding panicked, trying to find out if I had Kammegian's new cell phone number. When I dialed back to give it to him, there was no answer and no machine to record a message. Strange stuff, I thought, for someone like Doc who made his living using the telephone to not have a machine picking up his calls.

Sunday morning she still hadn't come back or telephoned from Vegas. I hadn't slept at all.

At eight o'clock, eating breakfast, Timothy could see that I was crazy. After I tried Laylonee's number and woke Mickey-o up and argued with him to find out there was no news, the boy began studying me with worried eyes. He had been through this deal before.

When I sat back down, he said he wanted to talk. He had come to a semi-decision, narrowed it down, and wanted my input. Who did I prefer, Tiger Woods or Mark McGwire?

I said that of course I preferred baseball. Mark McGwire.

Timothy looked unconvinced. He was now six years old, he said, and it was time to get started making preparations. Did I know that Tiger Woods began his career as a golfer at three years old? Did I know that he was an expert putter by the time he was seven?

The diversion was fine with me. With nothing to do but wait anyway, we hashed it through and determined that the best course of action was hands-on research. We got dressed and drove to The Sports Chalet in Marina del Rey.

Once in the store, it turned out to be no contest. McGwire won hands down. For Timothy, seeing the golf balls, then lousing up several attempts at putting them correctly, was the determining factor. We bought him two new bats, a box of baseballs, and a new, autographed Mark McGwire glove. On our way back home, parking in the garage, I returned to the subject of his mom and what he wanted to do. The boy shook his head. It was no big deal. He was used to it.

Monday morning and still no Jimmi. Because of the kid, I had no choice but to report late for work. I knew it would mean taking heat from Eddy Kammegian for my tardiness, but the boy had to be dropped off at his YMCA day camp. It didn't open until after six o'clock. On the street in front of my apartment, we loaded his bats and his mit and his backpack into my Chrysler, and we were on our way.

Once I had let him out, it was ten minutes across Lincoln to the Orbit Computer Products parking lot.

Pulling in on the gravel driveway, I got a jolt; everybody was outside. The entire staff. A stream of yellow police tape criss-crossed the fancy doorway of Orbit Computer Products. Two cops stood barring the entrance.

A big guy in a suit, someone I had never seen before, was

holding court, standing on one of the smokers' benches against the building. I locked my car and walked across the gravel.

When Frankie Freebase saw me join the crowd, he pulled me aside. 'Hey Dante,' he whispered, 'I hope you cashed your fucking paycheck on Friday.'

'What's up?' I shot back, trying to ignore him and hear what was being said, checking the faces of the others in the crowd for answers.

'Up!' Freebase sneered, now a foot from my nose, 'the fucking Boniventure hotel is up! Mount Whitney is up! Eddy-glorious-fucking-kami-kazi-Kammegian's time is up! Him and your buddy, the Doctor of Love – that lying fucking douchebag cocksucker! His time is up too. They're out on bail and you and me and all of us are out of a job. Standing here listening to some jerkoff with our dicks in our hands. That's what's up!'

'Okay. Why? What happened?'

'C'mon asshole, you'n me should talk. Let's go. I'll buy you breakfast. This putz cop has been rambling on for half the morning about the telemarketing task force and interstate phone fraud, and the fucking Free Trade Act. Like it all fucking matters now. Like any of it means dogshit now.'

I pushed him away. 'I'm staying. I work here.'

Frankie grabbed my arm. 'Kammegian called me Friday night from the Twin Towers lock up. I spoke to him myself. You wanna know what happened? What went down? Come with me!'

We got in Frankie Freebase's new Porsche and drove to Denny's Coffee Shop on Lincoln Boulevard, three minutes away.

I was still mostly sleepless and stunned, trying to make sense out of what I had just seen.

Freebase ordered a hot fudge sundae. He told the waitress he was having eggs after that. 'Whaddya havin', hotshot?'

'Coffee.'

'Coffee for the hotshot,' he said to the waitress. 'On me.'

I blew my nose in a napkin, still stupid from lack of sleep.

'You want a job, Dante? I'm opening my own boiler room. First National Copier Products. I been makin' calls all weekend. Good name, right? Catchy. By next Monday, I'll have a lease and the phones'll be up. My own joint. Fuckin' guaranteed!'

'What happened to Eddy and Doc?'

'Are you still sober? You look like shit. If you're back on the juice, forget the offer.'

'What happened, goddamn it?'

'Bribery, my man. Kickbacks and fucking payoffs. Federal indictments. Kammegian and Doctor Dickless and his best rectal buddy, Miltie Butler, at American Farmers Insurance. All busted. I got it from the horse's mouth.'

'C'mon! Eddy had nothing to do with that. You know him.'

'Orbit's been rakin' in five hundred thousand dollars a year from American Farmers. Ever think Kammegian mighta been lookin' the other way? Question, smart guy: How come Milt Butler was paying the highest prices in the fucking industry?'

'I don't know. Doc's a good salesman.'

'Right. Sure. Blow me. Eight weeks ago the fuckin' bean counters on the fifty-sixth floor at AFI mandate Butler to cut back on his monster fucking supply orders. Right?'

'Okay.'

'Then, surprise surprise, on the last day of the fuckin' Paris contest, Doctor dogshit strolls in with a seventy-nine thousand dollar order. Wake up, asshole! Two and two don't make fuckin' seven.'

'I don't care. I don't believe it.'

'I been bustin' my hump and gettin' short-sticked for the

last three years. Those cocksuckers got what was comin' to 'em.'

'Eddy Kammegian wasn't involved. I'm sure of it.'

'You're like a kid, Dante. A mooch. You want a hero: go rent a Stallone movie. Best any of us ever gets is sober. Kammegian forgot that. He's no better than you and me. Just sicker and more fucking powerful and way more out of control. That motherfucker ain't Jesus, man. And I, Frankie Freebase, am sittin' here lookin' you in the fuckin' face and tellin' you that Eddy-horse-neck-Kammegian didn't want to fuckin' know. But, like I said, it don't matter. Either way, Orbit is fah-mished, kaput, a fuckin' history book.'

My coffee came, and the hot fudge sundae, and Frankie's eggs for dessert.

He was leering at me. Across the table, his thousand dollar double-breasted suit made him look like a magazine ad for a rich prick. 'How about it, Bruno? You and me. You'll be the first employee at First National Copier Products.'

I stood up, dug in my pocket and dropped a dollar on the table. 'No deal, Frank. But have a swell day.'

At three o'clock, I was waiting outside the YMCA day camp for Timothy. When he came out, he opened the car door and began unloading his backpack and baseball equipment. 'Hey,' I said, noticing his stuff, 'you're missing one of your new bats.'

'I know,' he half-whispered, 'it broke.'

'A brand new bat! A twenty-nine dollar bat. Did you save the pieces? I'll return it to the store and get my money back.'

'Shit happens, Bruno.'

'Hey kid, language!'

'You say it. I've heard you.'

'Rules. Remember? I'm the adult.'

'You're correct. I apologize.'

As I was unlocking my apartment door, the phone rang. Timothy ran across the living room to get it. As soon as he picked it up, I knew it was her. His expression said it. They talked for a minute then he held the phone up. 'It's Mom. She needs to speak to you.'

The voice on the other end was tense and scared. 'Yo Bruno, it's me. I got trouble. Bad shit, baby.'

'Are you okay?'

'I'm gonna do a year, man! Mandatory. I got violated. My probation. I'm screwed.'

'What happened?'

'I was with some people who had dope in their car, and smoke, and some other shit. We got pulled over on the strip. They searched everybody.'

'Did you have cocaine on you?'

'I need money. Right away. Two thousand. One of the girls got a sharp drug attorney guy here in Vegas. He tole us to say the search waz illegal, you know?'

'But you still violated probation.'

'Are you listening to me, man?'

'They closed Orbit today, Jimmi. My company. I lost my job.'

'Hey, I'm on the fuckin' jail phone here! I need help! Jou got two grand or not?'

'Sure.'

'Send it. Don' come here and bring it. Jus wire it. Get a pencil, I'll give you where to mail the money.'

'What about Timothy? What happens to the kid?'

'Call my sister Sema. Tell her I'm in jail. She'll take him. She got no choice, man.'

I was watching the boy. He stood across the living room

by the window, listening, pretending to be looking out at the ocean.

Covering the phone's mouthpiece with my hand, I called to him. 'Hey,' I said, 'It looks like Jimmi might not be coming back soon. Do you want to go back to your Aunt Sema's house?'

He wouldn't answer. Finally, slowly, he shook his head 'no.' His voice was barely audible. 'If it's alright with you, I want to stay here. Is that okay?'

He had his mother's eyes. Blue. As blue as the world's deepest, bluest sky. 'You'd have to sleep in your own bed,' I said. 'In *your* bedroom.'

The boy was smiling. 'That would be okay, Bruno. I would consider that an acceptable compromise.'

I was back on the phone. 'Look Jimmi,' I said, something caught in my throat, 'I'm sorry . . . I have to go now.'

Then I hung up the phone.

CHUMP CHANGE
A novel by
DAN FANTE

A New York winter - and the devil has you by the balls.

At the end of a Mad Dog binge you set about yourself with a steak knife. Released from the nut ward they were reluctant to sling you in, your wife takes time out from her affair with a fitness instructor to tell you your father's in a coma – limbless, blind and dumb.

You get yourself to LA for a fraught family reunion and soon realise the only way to get through this hell involves more booze. A couple of days later you wake up naked in a stolen car with an underage hooker whose pimp has robbed you blind. Your father is about to die.

You are Bruno Dante. It's time for *Chump Change*.

'*Don't miss* Chump Change. *It is passionate, obscene and quite wonderful.*' Los Angeles Times

ISBN 1 84195 069 6   £10.00 pbk

You can order direct from
Canongate Books
14 High Street
Edinburgh EH1 1TE
Tel (0131) 557 5111 Fax (0131) 557 5211

Or from our website:
www.canongate.net

John Fante titles available as Rebel Inc Classics:

The Road to Los Angeles
With an introduction by John King
"Tender and lyrical ... its humour is wry and forgiving and its stylistic energy compelling."
The Guardian
1 84195 049 1   £6.99 pbk

Wait Until Spring, Bandini
With an introduction by Dan Fante
"Bandini is a magnificent creation, and his rediscovery is not before time." *Times Literary Supplement*
0 86241 978 6   £6.99 pbk

Ask the Dust
With an introduction by Charles Bukowski
"A tough and beautifully realised tale ... affecting, powerful and poignant stuff." *Time Out*
0 86241 839 9   £6.99 pbk

To order, or to find out more about
Rebel Inc Classics, visit our website:
www.canongate.net